WINGNUT

Operation Payback

L.R. BAKER

Order this book online at www.trafford.com
or email orders@trafford.com

Most Trafford titles are also available at major online book retailers.

Printed in the United States of America.

ISBN: 978-1-4269-5660-7 (sc)
ISBN: 978-1-4269-5661-4 (hc)
ISBN: 978-1-4269-5662-1 (e)

Libray of Congress Control Number: 2011902474

Trafford rev. 02/25/2014

 www.trafford.com

North America & international
toll-free: 1 888 232 4444 (USA & Canada)
fax: 812 355 4082

For Angelique, Owen and Michelle Baker: A legacy

Illustrations by
Vivienne Jones

PREFACE

This book was written solely from childhood memories from 1960-1963, in Christchurch, New Zealand.

The story is a work of fiction, based on real events as I remember them.

The characters described in the book are fictional.

ACKNOWLEDGEMENTS

I wish to acknowledge some of the people involved in my childhood that contributed to the memories from which I wrote this book:
Barry Toomey, Raymond Pye, Brian Williams, Judith McLennan, Donald Baker, and my parents, Des and Betty Baker.

I would like to thank all of the people who encouraged me with their interest and enthusiasm to complete this book, especially Michael and Ariana Corbet, who were the first children to have this story read to them (until they fell asleep that is), and Desmond Palmer, who has been waiting enthusiastically for a copy of this book.

CHAPTER 1

Wingnut is a small boy about 10 years old, who lives in the untidy, old, gray house next to the church at the end of my street. It is the only house on the street with no lawn, garden or driveway. It has a waist-high concrete wall across the front yard and it looks as though neither it, nor the house, has ever been painted in my lifetime.

My brother said that people call him Wingnut because of his big, sticky-out ears. I felt kind of sorry for him, but he really does look like one of those threaded nuts that I have on my bike, with the tabs on the side, so that you don't need a wrench to tighten them up. I often see him playing imaginary games by himself out on the street, when I ride my bike home from school. He always wears the same gray cotton shorts that look one size too small, and a dark blue shirt that looks one size too big. I have never seen him wear anything else on his feet, except black rubber gumboots with the tops turned down. I thought that perhaps he doesn't have any other clothes to wear, because he wears the same thing every day, winter and summer. I can't help thinking that his socks must get awfully stinky inside those boots on a hot day.

I have a pair of gummies like that too. I don't wear them every day but when I do, my socks really stink and they get a kind of stiff and crusty feeling. My brother gets mad when I leave them lying on the floor of the bedroom for a few days, especially when he can catch a whiff of them from his bed.

One day, I put them inside his pillow case, and when he went to bed that night he couldn't figure out where the strange smell was coming from. He kept getting out of bed to search underneath it for cat poop, with his flashlight. Eventually, feeling the lump in his pillow, he ripped them out and dove over to my bed with them clutched in his hand, and vigorously rubbed them all over my face.

I was screaming and yelling, and trying to fight him off, when Mom came storming into the room, grabbed him by the ear, and marched him into the hall for a slap on the bum and a good yelling at. I could hear her shrieking at the top of her voice, how she has had just about enough of our stupid pranks. I was thinking that if she has had "just" about enough, that could mean the same as not quite enough, so one or two more practical jokes probably wouldn't hurt. Mom snapped me out of my daydream with a screeching tongue whip, which lashed down upon me as I put my head under the covers and pretended to go to sleep. She didn't appreciate that prank very much, either.

My brother said that he would get me back for getting him in trouble. Since he is four years older than me, I'm sure he will. So I had better be careful for a couple of days.

Balancing on the wall

I saw Wingnut again a couple of days later, as I rode my bike home from school. He was playing by himself as usual, still wearing the same shorts, shirt and gumboots. He was walking along the top of the wall in front of his house,

3

pausing to balance on one leg, while waving his arms about. I thought that he was probably pretending to be a circus tightrope walker or something. Anyway, there he was, silly little Wingnut, balancing on one leg on top of the wall, having a great time by himself, in his imagination. As I rode by, he caught sight of me from the corner of his eye, turned his head suddenly, and started to frantically windmill his skinny arms in opposite directions. His mouth was open and his eyes were open extra wide, nearly popping out of his head. He teetered there for a few seconds, looking very funny indeed, and then suddenly he just fell off onto the sidewalk. He didn't get up, cry or make a sound; he just lay there thrashing about on the ground. I thought that he should be a circus clown, always fooling about like that.

I just kept pedaling my bike down the road. After a minute or so, as I turned into my driveway, I looked back and saw that Wingnut was still lying on the sidewalk. I turned my bike around and rode back to find him lying on his side, curled up in a ball, clutching his leg, and making weird moaning sounds.

"Are you alright?" I asked.

Talking through his clenched teeth he said,

"No, my leg really hurts. I think I've got a bruise."

As I tried to help him up, he whimpered some more. I thought that the bruise must be a big one, so I picked him up and carried him to his front door. All the paint had been worn off around the doorknob, and a big patch was worn off at the bottom, where many shoes had kicked it open. So I kicked it in the same spot, trying to make it sound like a knock, as

I had my hands full of whimpering Wingnut. My legs were beginning to tremble with the strain; he wasn't a big kid but it seemed that his weight was doubling each second. Finally, Wingnut's big fat mother, with her strange teeth and weird haircut, opened the door. She just gave me a come-inside nod with her head, so I followed her into the house and at the next head nod, I laid Wingnut down on the cluttered couch. Then she made a freaky sound like a seal barking and nodded towards the door. I figured it was definitely time to make a dash for my bike, and pedaled home as fast as I could.

My mom is on a diet, so for some reason we all have to be on a diet. I really miss our ordinary food; now we have to eat salad, bean sprouts, and raw vegetables and stuff like that. My dad doesn't like it much either, but he never says anything, he just sits there and eats it. My brother sometimes complains. One day he even left the table, and started cooking himself something else. For the next two weeks he had no dinner served to him at all—he had to make his own dinner every day. Anyway, these diet things never seem to last long. All it takes is for someone to come over for a visit, with a cake or homemade cookies or something, and the diet deal is off.

That night my brother, sister and I listened to our favorite serial on the radio. Mom let us stay up a little later than usual to listen to a new series of stories. The radio was placed in a proud position in our living room, on a shelf above the new record player. We knew of a family a few streets away that had a television set in their living room. We all thought, Wow! How fantastic must that be? The new radio serial was a comedy show about a family and several other silly characters.

We have been waiting for this series to come on the radio since last year. Now that it is finally November 1960, it is here at last. It was a very funny show, and we all laughed from beginning to end. When it was over, Mom presented the three of us a chocolate biscuit each. It was a special treat, as cookies were heavily guarded by the cookie jailer, and were kept stashed away in a secret place. We all knew where they were of course, but we never dared take any without asking, because the punishment for such a terrible crime was dealt out quickly and severely. It was never the same; depending on the particular mood of the cookie custodian, it could range from a whack on the head, to a brutal yelling at, or perhaps crucifixion on a cross, or even banishment from the universe. So if we actually wanted to play, any time in the rest of our lives, we left the forbidden cookies alone.

We all got washed and ready for bed. Mom herded us all into the bathroom to brush our teeth with salt, which had been lovingly blended with water to create a truly revolting toothpaste. My toothbrush was made of wood. The bristles had been folded in half over little brass tabs and jammed into the little holes in the head of the brush, to hold them in place.

One day, when I was half asleep, I was brushing my teeth vigorously, trying to get it over with as soon as possible, when all the little brass tabs decided to fall out.

It took me a second or two to figure out what the heck was happening to me, as my mouth filled with prickly bristles. It felt like I was having one of those terrible nightmares, where you get stuck in thick mud, or have lots of sand in your eyes, or you suddenly find yourself standing in front of your entire class completely naked.

I began to gag, cough and wrestle my tongue around these things, trying to spit them out. It took ages to find the last of the bristles up under my lip, and flick it out with my finger. The neat thing of it all was that the next day I got a new, bright blue, plastic toothbrush, which felt super smooth in my mouth after the old wooden one.

Because of the smelly socks trick, and my brother's pledge to get even, that night I carefully checked to see if the bottom of my pyjama legs had been stapled together, or if my sheets had been folded back two feet too short, or if miscellaneous foreign objects had been placed in my pillow or bed. When I was totally convinced that my bed was quite safe and free from booby traps or tricks, I got in between the nice clean, white sheets that had been hung outside on the clothesline in the sun to dry, after my mom had done the laundry. I loved the clean, fresh smell and feel of newly washed sheets; it was almost as nice as stuffing my face into a pile of hot linen that Mom had just ironed. I gave my pillow one last security sniff just to make sure, and then fell into a lovely dream-filled sleep.

Sometime in the night, I was dreaming that I was having a pee. I was standing on the top of the stone wall outside Wingnut's house, peeing onto the sidewalk. I was just standing there with my pee pee in my hand, peeing and peeing. Suddenly, I woke with a shock. After a moment or two, I realized that I was soaking wet from head to foot. I thought, "Oh no, I've wet the bed and Mom said that I wouldn't get my allowance if I peed the bed again." She said that I was much too old for that. I thought I was too old for that too, as I hadn't done that for about a year. Perhaps if I got up, stripped the sheets off the bed, got new pyjamas, and stuffed all the wet stuff into the washing machine, she wouldn't notice. Feeling that this was a great idea, I got out of bed and started pulling off the sheets. My brother woke and seemed to be quietly snickering to himself. I asked him what he thought was so funny.

"Nothing," he said, and pretended to go back to sleep. Mom heard me moving about, and came into our room in her dressing gown, with huge, pink curlers in her hair. I never quite figured out exactly what they were supposed to do, but she seemed to like them, as she wore them nearly every night. She said,

"What on earth are you doing in here in the middle of the night?" Since I was totally caught in the act of stripping off the sheets, I had to confess to peeing in my bed. She sighed her huge sigh saying that she thought I had passed that stage. As she came over towards my bed in her bare feet, she suddenly stopped, looked down, lifted up her foot and examined the stuff that was stuck to the bottom of it. She said,

"What on earth have you spilled in here now?" I told her that I hadn't spilled anything. But I could see her eyebrows starting to rise, and her overall expression began to take on the stern and ready-to-explode look.

"It's salt! How did you get salt sprinkled all over the floor? I told you, no eating in the bedroom. Why do you always disobey me?"

From the bed on the other side of the room, we both heard a muffled snicker. Mom strode over there in two seconds.

"What do you know about this, mister? And exactly what do you find so funny?"

"Nothing," my brother said. Mom stomped back to my bed, grasped her fingers around the edge of the bottom bed sheet and ripped it off with a flourish, like a magician doing the magic tablecloth trick.

There, under my sheet, was a layer of white, soggy, gooey gunk. My mom touched it, suddenly spun around on her heel, and strode out the door at high speed with her dressing gown flapping behind her in the breeze she created, and the curlers dancing a jig on top her head. My brother suddenly sat up in bed, looking a little worried. The giggling had definitely stopped for some reason, and he didn't seem to think that things were quite so funny anymore.

Mom finds the salt box

Mom appeared in the doorway, like a pop-up figure at an amusement park that suddenly jumps up and scares the living daylights out of people. She was clutching an empty saltbox, which was upside down with the lid open.

"Explain this!" she screeched, as she furiously shook the empty box at my brother.

He had sprinkled the entire box of salt under my sheet, spreading it all over the bed in a nice even layer. As I slept, the salt soaked up the moisture from my body and soaked everything, including me. He experienced his very first midnight spanking and was grounded until he grew up, got married and moved out.

CHAPTER 2

Every day, as I rode home from school, I looked for wee Wingnut as I passed his house. I hadn't seen him for three or four days. We were all sitting at the dinner table eating some ghastly diet mixture Mom had made. It was brown and sloppy with big lumps of soggy stuff floating around in it. Mom asked Dad if he liked his tofu; he took a long sip of his beer and just nodded. My sister said that someone in her class told her that a kid on our street was taken to the hospital with a broken leg a few days ago.

"Wingnut!" I exclaimed.

"Who on earth is Wingnut?" Mom asked. I told her that he is a kid at the end of our street who doesn't have any friends. I told them all how I had seen him fall off the wall, and how I had carried him into his house, and heard the weird barking sound his mother had made.

The next day after school, Mom made us have a wash, change our clothes and get into the car. She told us that we were going to the hospital to visit the mysterious Wingnut.

Ward 3 was where Wingnut was supposed to be, in the children's ward. It seemed to be a long way from the front entrance of the hospital, as we walked down lots of hallways to get there. Mom said that she didn't think that Wingnut had had any visitors at all since he had been in here. Probably not even his mom, brothers or sisters. She also said that she had heard that Wingnut's dad died when Wingnut was only five, and his mom was very poor, and almost never left the house. Mom asked the nurse which bed Graham was in, when we reached the door of Ward 3.

"Is his real name Graham?" I asked.

"Yes" she said, "at least that's what Mrs. Smith from across the street told me."

Wingnut was lying on his back on a bed covered with crumpled sheets and small comic books. The comics were all World War II stories, and Wingnut seemed to have plenty of them.

Mom cleared her throat as we approached, which was a very useful sound when she wanted to get someone's attention. Wingnut looked up at all of us standing in a row, at the side of his bed. He recognized me.

"Hi! Did you all come here to see me?" he asked.

"Yes," we all chimed, simultaneously. His eyes lit up, and a huge smiley grin began to grow from the centre of his face and spread out towards each side, forcing his ears to move up and back at the same time. His right leg was in a huge plaster cast, from his toes to his hip, and it was hoisted up at a steep angle by a pulley attached to a frame on his bed.

He had a bed sheet covering his left leg, pulled up to his chest. The plastered right leg was brilliant white, brand new plaster. My sister said,

"Can we sign your cast?" Wingnut smiled that expanding smile again and said,

"Sure. I have a pen right here."

As he twisted himself around to reach the pen on his bedside table, the bed sheet moved with him, and my sister, who had moved closer to the bed to do the signing, suddenly jumped back a little, as Wingnut's little pee pee peaked out from under the sheet as it moved. She started to giggle and point.

Soon we all realized what was so funny, and we all began giggling loudly too.

Wingnut looked at us all, grinned, pulled the sheet back over himself and said,

"Oh! That happens sometimes, because I don't have any one-legged pyjamas." At that, we all laughed like mad, and took turns signing the smooth white plaster cast.

We had all been forbidden to play any tricks or pull any pranks on each other, especially at bedtime, so when we got home that night it was actually quite nice to get into my bed without having to check it over for booby traps.

I visited Wingnut several more times while he was in hospital. Mom had a friend in the women's ward that she visited at the same time. I hated to go with her, as there was absolutely nothing for me to do there while Mom sat and nattered with this lady that I didn't even know. I could never figure out what on earth they were talking about, and

I certainly couldn't figure out why it took so terribly long to say it. I was always so bored just sitting in a chair while Mom and the lady talked and talked and talked.

I found a piece of string in the corridor and spent the entire time playing with that piece of string, tying and untying it to my chair.

The lady had hoses up her nose, which gave me the willies to look at her. I had never seen that before and didn't exactly know what they were for. On our third visit to the hospital, Mom said that it would be OK if I visited with Wingnut while she went to visit her friend on the women's ward. I was so thrilled not to have to go with her; I could hardly wait until she left.

Time flew by as I sat on Wingnut's bed, while he gave me a guided tour of his impressive war comic collection. He said that I could take some of them home with me if I would like. I chose three of them and put them inside my shirt. He also let me have some of his chocolates, which were in the drawer of his bedside table.

As we talked, our conversation drifted back to the day when he fell off the wall. He told me that he was pretending to be a Zulu chief doing a war dance, to rally his warriors and incite them to rise up and wage war, to defeat the evil Shulaks.

He had such passion and emotion in his voice, I thought that he was going to leap out of bed and massacre the first Shulak he came upon.

"Who the heck are the evil Shulaks? Are they an African Zulu tribe from one of your war comics?" I asked him innocently.

"No, no, no. You know the two Shulaks, don't you? The two redheaded, freckle-faced bullies that go to our school?"

"Do you go to my school?" I exclaimed in surprise.

"Of course I do, I live in the same neighbourhood don't I?"

"Yes, but whose class are you in? And how come I never see you at school?"

Wingnut went on to explain how he had moved into our neighbourhood a year ago, and was put back a year at school because he wasn't doing very well since he had failed his exams at the end of the last year. He was in a class at the other end of the school, and even ate his lunch in a totally different part of the school than me. I asked him why he is always home before me, changed out of his school clothes and playing outside, while I am still riding my bike home. He said,

"I beat all the kids home from school, because I take my secret shortcut. As soon as the bell rings, I take off across the back playing fields before anyone sees me. I run straight across the open fields as fast as I can, to reach the top of the small hill on the other side. Once I reach the hill and I am safely down the other side, then I can relax."

"Aren't you scared that the teachers will see you, or that you will be attacked by the magpies nesting in the giant pine trees surrounding the playing fields? That's why the fields are out of bounds at this time of year, because the magpies will land on your head with their claws in your hair, lean over your face, and try to peck your eyes out!"

"No!" he said, "I have my automatic, rotating magpie stick stashed in a hollow tree trunk near the school back gate. When I get across the park, I stash it under the big prickly hedge, and then in the morning, I pick it up, run across the fields and put it back in the tree trunk."

"Why do you risk getting into trouble by going to a place that is designated out of bounds for the school kids?" I asked.

"Well, it's safer than meeting up with the dreaded Shulaks" he said sternly. "Besides, I always see neat things; every day I see something different on my secret shortcut."

"The day I broke my leg, I saw a live eel swimming in the small weed-filled ditch, which has only about eight inches of water in it. I tried to catch it but it got away on me. I'll bet the two of us could get it, if one of us blocked its path while the other hooked it out of the water. If we could catch it we could light a fire, cook it on a stick, and eat it. I tried eel once and it tastes as good as any other fish. I also saw a dead hedgehog in the drain that runs beside the little ditch. You see," Wingnut went on to explain,

"The drain is a concrete culvert that always has about six inches of water in it, except when it rains; all of the rain water from the storm gutters on the surrounding streets drains into it, filling it almost to the top. It has straight concrete sides about five feet deep and a concrete bottom. The bottom has a coating of green slime on it, but it's OK to walk in there, if you have your gummies on. It's just wide enough to jump across, but you have to run as fast as you can before jumping, or you'll never make it across. If you miss, you'll crash into the concrete on the other side, and probably fall into the mucky water."

"How do you get out, if you are paddling in there in your gumboots?" I inquired.

"Well, you have to walk along until you come to one of the gutter pipes that appear as holes in the concrete sides of the drain. You can put the toe of your boot in the hole and use it as a step to climb out." Wingnut said that any animals that fell in there just starved to death or drowned, because they couldn't get out. He said that the hedgehog he saw had fallen in, and swam up and down until it finally got exhausted, and drowned.

He said that it was all squishy, bloated up and covered with flies, and floating in the water. He went on to tell me that every once in a while the city council sends convicts from the prison to clean it out, guarding them with rifles from the narrow track that runs through the long grass between the drain and the little ditch. He said that there is a huge, prickly hedge that runs down each side, and it continues for miles and miles. It goes past the back of the school, all the way to the estuary that runs into the sea. At the very end of the drain, he said there are huge old wooden gates that are supposed to stop the water from backing up into the drain when there is a flood or a very high tide.

"One day," he declared, "I am going to walk all the way down the drain to see those flood gates."

Suddenly a loud bell rang, and an announcement blared out over the intercom system. The voice on the speaker was full of authority and firmly declared that hospital visiting hours will be over in five minutes.

Wingnut gave me another one of his chocolates and thanked me for visiting him.

Mom appeared in the doorway and announced that we should get moving, to avoid the rush. I said goodbye to Wingnut, stuffed my three war comics securely into the top of my pants on the inside of my shirt, and Mom and I joined the flow of people that came pouring out from all the rooms, filling the hallways.

I thought of the drain, with all its storm gutter pipes, pouring water into it during a rainstorm. The flow of people increased more and more, as all the people visiting tried to leave the hospital at the same time.

The whole situation was made worse by some of the mobile patients insisting on coming to the main door to see their visitors off. Many of them were either in wheelchairs, on crutches or trundling funny stands with bottles of fluid hanging and jiggling from them.

I thought of the drain again with all the bits of wood, dead animals and assorted garbage, flowing down its restricted channel to the sea.

That night, after listening to the stories on the radio, I raced to be the first to get washed and ready for bed. I brushed my teeth with some new toothpaste that Mom had bought. It was in a tube that was carefully rolled up from the bottom as the toothpaste got used up.

Mom gave us all instructions on the correct way to use this new toothpaste: how much to use, and how to squeeze the tube only from the bottom, and always to put the cap back on when you are done.

I said goodnight to everyone. My brother was staying up to listen to another story on the radio that Mom had said was on too late for me. My brother was four years older, so he was allowed to stay up later. I didn't mind, as I really didn't like those late stories anyway. The last time I stayed up and listened to them when Mom and Dad had gone out for the evening, I had really bad nightmares, as the stories were very scary and I didn't like them at all.

I had the bedroom all to myself, and with the door shut, I retrieved the three war comics that were still tangled up in my shirt. I chose one and put the other two in between some larger books that were on a shelf under my bedside table.

The books there were all new ones that my grandmother and auntie had given me for Christmas.

The teacher at school said that I wasn't doing very well with my reading, and that I should be reading for at least an hour each day. The problem is, I don't actually have an hour, as all my hours are used up with other things and I just don't have any hours left over.

I don't really have anything to read either, because my new books are thick and would probably take me the rest of my life to read. One is called *Robinson Crusoe* and the other is called *Treasure Island*. Perhaps I will look at them one day, as the pictures look fairly interesting. Perhaps they would have been good to take to the hospital to read while I was sitting there waiting for Mom to stop talking.

Anyway, I started to look at Wingnut's war comic. It was titled "Operation Payback." It was just my size, twenty pages with lots of pictures. All the words were in little cloudlike balloons with a pointed end, directed at who said what in the story. I read the entire comic before my brother came to bed. I was feeling very sleepy by the time I was done, as I am not used to reading for very long.

It was an exciting story about six British army soldiers who had been ordered to deliver four trucks, loaded with valuable supplies, to an isolated army camp that had been cut off from the rest of the army. The soldiers were under heavy enemy gunfire, day and night.

Without the supplies of food, guns and ammunition, they would all certainly be slaughtered by the approaching German soldiers within a few days. The British army had tried to send several convoys of trucks to rescue the trapped soldiers, but there was only one road through the mountain pass that led to the camp.

Every time they sent trucks through the pass, they would be ambushed by a small group of well-hidden Germans who were perched high up on a hill, overlooking the road.

The Germans, hidden in the hills, fired upon any British army vehicles that tried to get through.

The six brave British soldiers, who had been assigned to drive the trucks through the pass, in one last desperate attempt to save their comrades, devised a cunning plan.

They had been told that the soldiers in the previous trucks couldn't defend themselves, because they never knew exactly where the hail of bullets had come from, as the Germans in the hills were so well-hidden. Their weapons were aimed at the road in advance, so when the trucks passed by, they only fired short, furious bursts of gunfire at the helpless trucks, then immediately stopped. The British couldn't tell exactly where they were located and therefore, could not fire back.

The war comic

The six men repaired one of the shot-up trucks that had survived a previous attack. It was badly damaged, but they managed to patch it up, and after a new coat of paint it looked like new from a distance. They spent an entire day welding steel plates into the cab of the truck. The plates would protect the driver from German bullets.

The driver could sit inside the steel box they had constructed, and look out through the small narrow slot they had cut in the front.

On the outside of the driver's small armoured box, they painted the figure of a man sitting holding a steering wheel. It looked as though you could see the entire inside of the truck cab, with the driver sitting in full view, but actually, he was well hidden behind the walls of the steel box in which he sat.

The six men agreed that they would draw straws to see who would drive their patched-up, modified creation. The plan that they had devised was to drive three supply-laden trucks all the way to the entrance of the mountain pass, with the fourth modified truck being towed behind, with only enough fuel to drive about two miles.

The plan was to then drive that truck up to the front of the convoy to travel alone into the pass, in full view of the ambushing Germans. The other three trucks were to remain hidden among the trees and bushes, out of sight of the enemy.

At dawn the next morning, the trucks set off on their life-or-death mission. Three of the trucks were heavily laden with weapons, ammunition, food and supplies, with the fourth under tow, completely empty, except for the driver to steer it.

They traveled slowly because of their heavy loads, and they reached the entrance of the pass about two hours before nightfall. The three lead trucks pulled off the road and parked out of sight among the trees. The drivers then unloaded three bazookas, five machine guns and as many hand grenades as they could carry, and hastily disappeared up the tree-covered slope that formed the sides of the mountain pass.

Just as the last rays of sunshine faded into dusk, they looked down onto the road to see their decoy truck, trundling along the road in the silent warm breeze of the early evening.

Shattering the silence, a ferocious barrage of gunfire startled the five soldiers into action. The blast was shockingly intense, but only lasted for about twenty seconds. The five men could all clearly see the smoke from the gunfire, drifting off in the breeze. They could also see the German guns, still smoking from the heat of the savage workout they had just had.

The five men were higher up the hillside than the Germans, hidden in their well-camouflaged bunker, which had been made of old logs and rocks. The men were so close, they could hear the enemy laughing and congratulating each other.

"Time to wipe the smiles off their faces, lads," the leader said, and the five men silently spread out, positioning themselves at good vantage points above the enemy.

At the sound of the leader's whistle, the three bazookas and two machine guns fired simultaneously in a fast and furious payback.

The pass was now safe for the soldiers and their trucks to pass through, to rescue all the brave men who were helplessly trapped at the other end.

The soldier who drove the decoy truck was unharmed, but his ears rang for three days from the racket of the bullets slamming into the steel box around him.

CHAPTER 3

Mom told me Wingnut was discharged from hospital, but he wasn't back at school yet. She said he would be at home another few weeks, as he needed to get the big cast off his leg and get a smaller, lighter one to wear to school.

I didn't see Wingnut again for quite a long time. I had thought about going to his house to see him, but I was scared of his freaky mother.

One day I caught sight of Wingnut at school. He was sitting on the ground in the school courtyard eating his lunch. I walked over and sat down with him. He seemed glad to see me and offered me a potato. I shook my head, no, and he promptly began eating it raw just like an apple. He said,

"I have three of them. Are you sure you don't want one?"

"No," I said, "I don't think that I would like potato raw."

"Oh, they're good!" he said. "I have them for lunch every day."

"That's all?" I asked.

"Oh no," he replied enthusiastically, "I have a piece of bread with butter on it, too."

Poor Wingnut. I thought about having raw potato and bread for lunch every day. I don't think that I will complain about my bologna and cheese sandwiches ever again.

At the end of the lunch break, I told him that I had read all of his war comics and that I thought they were great stories. He said,

"Why don't you meet me at the school back gate after the bell rings, and take my secret shortcut with me and I will give you more of them to read."

It was a hot, dry, windy day and dust was blowing up from the gravel pathway that formed a border around the entire park. There were no people around except for an old man with a dog, way off in the distance.

The giant pine trees that grew all around the perimeter of the park, along the edge of the pathway, were waving and swaying in the wind. Spring pollen was blowing from the trees in light clouds of yellow dust. Every once in a while, a huge pine cone would crash to the ground in a cloud of falling needles that it had cracked loose during its fall to the ground.

The wind was hot, and the whole park had a spooky, edgy feeling about it. There were huge black magpies circling around high in the air, riding the wind with ease. There were also many magpies sitting on the very tops of the massive trees, doing nothing except watching Wingnut and me as we slipped quickly and quietly through the gate at the back of our school.

We stopped for a few minutes to tighten the straps of the school bags on our backs so that they wouldn't bounce up and down when we ran. We were standing under the cover of several big chestnut trees that were growing near the school gate, then Wingnut walked off, and was peering into a hole in the trunk of a dead tree.

"What are you doing?" I asked.

"I'm getting my magpie stick," he replied, and gave a groan of satisfaction as he grasped onto the stick, which was stashed at arm's length inside the hollow tree.

I remembered the story that Wingnut had told me when he was in the hospital, about the fierce magpies and his rotating stick. It was actually two sticks: one was a handle with a groove carved around it, and the other longer stick was fastened to the handle piece with an old lawn mower pull string. The long piece was about as long as my arm. Wingnut demonstrated how it worked by holding the handle up and swinging the stick rapidly above his head like a helicopter blade.

He said that magpies can't land on his head without getting whacked, as long as he keeps swinging the stick.

It was a long way to the far side of the park. Wingnut pointed out the patch of prickly bushes that were peeping out over the small hill in the distance. We were ready to make a run for the bushes when I realized to my dismay that we only had one stick.

For some reason, Wingnut thought this little detail was very funny. When he finally stopped laughing he said that we would just have to run shoulder-to-shoulder so we could both be under the protection of his stick. We counted: one, two, three. We raced off, darting out from the cover of the chestnut trees, into the open, with dust stirring up from our feet. The sun was hot and we were soon sweating from the exertion of our shoulder-to-shoulder run.

The magpie attack

"Here they come!" Wingnut shouted. I looked up to see about twenty large magpies launch themselves from the tree tops and plunge at high speed towards us. We were almost to the centre of the park, completely out in the open, and the magpies were getting closer and closer.

Down they swooped at startling speed, dive-bombing us, two or three at a time. With each swoop they took, they got closer to our heads. Wingnut was swinging the stick with all his might. I could hear it swishing through the air with each revolution.

Without warning, the string snapped and the rotating part flew off and went spinning off end over end, crashing onto the ground in a cloud of dust. Wingnut and I stared at each other with startled looks of horror and disbelief.

We both screamed and sprinted off with our hands clasped firmly on top of our heads. It was an awkward position for running and we were still very close together.

The magpies sensed our vulnerable state and dived down, screeching and trying to grab our hair with their sharp claws. I twisted sharply to avoid an attack, and our bodies crashed together. Our legs collided, and we both slammed into the ground in a tangled heap. We scrambled to our feet in seconds, but the magpies were upon us, clawing at our hair and pecking our heads in a flurry of flapping wings and high pitched squawking.

We were so terrified, we were dancing about like we were barefoot on a hot sandy beach, waving our arms about frantically, trying to fend off the attacking birds.

"Run for it!" Wingnut screamed, and we both fled as fast as possible, for the cover of bushes on the other side of the park. We sped over the little hill, leaped down the other side and lay in the grass under the thick bushes, panting and sweating.

The magpies had defended their territory to their satisfaction, and they all flew back to the treetops.

We lay in the grass for some time, catching our breath and recovering from our ordeal.

"So much for the automatic rotating magpie stick," I said. Wingnut burst out laughing, and then I started laughing, too.

"You should have seen the look on your face when that string broke. You looked like you suddenly realized that you'd crapped your pants when you thought that you'd only farted." Wingnut exploded into an uncontrollable laughing fit. He was rolling in the grass, laughing so hard he had to hold his stomach with both hands; tears of laughter were rolling down his cheeks. He stammered,

"You should have seen the look on your face when we fell down, and that magpie grabbed your hair. You looked like a cat with a string of fireworks tied to its tail!" We roared with laughter again, and didn't stop laughing until we were startled by a loud and very stern shout.

"Hey you kids!" It was the park caretaker, looking like he meant business, and he was heading in our direction.

"Let's go!" Wingnut shouted. "Run for it!" We leaped up and with Wingnut leading the way, we ran at full speed down the narrow trail that ran between the drain and the little ditch. The overgrown track had long grass and prickly leaves hanging over it, slashing and whipping at our legs as we ran.

We kept running as fast as we could without looking back. Suddenly my foot came down on something very squishy that popped and squelched as I stepped on it. I let out a frightened yelp and then was nearly overcome by a very foul stench. I glanced behind me and was horrified to see that I had stepped on a dead, bloated, drowned hedgehog that had been fished out of the drain and flung into the grass. The smell was terrible and as I looked down at my shoe I could see that it was splattered with rotten hedgehog guts and squirming maggots.

I let out another horrified yelp as I began frantically dragging my shoe sideways through the long grass in an effort to wipe off the disgusting mess. I picked up a small stick and picked and flicked off as much of the gunk as I could, then flung the stick into the grass in disgust.

Wingnut was laughing again, and gleefully exclaimed that he was glad he hadn't stepped on it.

We continued walking down the track at a leisurely pace after we noticed that the park caretaker had given up the chase. For the rest of the way home, I was very careful to watch where I was stepping.

Wingnut pointed out the place where he had seen the eel and he showed me the holes in the sides of the drain where the rain from the street gutters flowed into it. We reached the old fence, which crossed in front of us. It was made of fencing wire with a big wooden post across the top that had several strands of barbed wire nailed to it to stop people from climbing over it.

The drain ran under the road through a square tunnel and disappeared into the blackness. We could hear a strange gurgling sound coming from the depths of the tunnel, but it was so dark in there that you couldn't see anything.

Wingnut said that he had heard the noise before and we both sat on the side of the drain with our legs dangling over the edge, contemplating what the spooky, gurgling sound might be.

First we thought of trolls, lurking in the darkness waiting for some nice boys to eat.

Then images of swamp creatures, or perhaps an insane escaped prisoner who had hidden himself in there one day when they were cleaning the drain out, and who has been in there ever since, and only comes out at night.

We sat on the edge of the drain for quite some time talking and imagining what the gurgling sound might be.

The sound of a car, as it crossed over the hump in the road that was created by the drain passing under it, brought us back to reality.

"Come on," Wingnut said. "Let's go to my house. I said I would give you some more war comics."

Because of all the running we had been doing on the way home from school, first through the park then along the drain, I figured that it must be fairly early, and that Mom wouldn't be home yet, so I agreed to go to Wingnut's house to get some more war comics.

We walked side by side down the deserted sidewalk in the afternoon sun, reminiscing about the adventures we had just had. We were both looking fairly dirty, as we had a lot of dust stuck to us from our tumble in the park. My shoe still had splotches of hedgehog guts on it and Wingnut said that I could use his garden hose to wash it off when we got to his house.

We could see some of the school kids on their way home, riding their bikes along the avenue that crossed the exit of our street. Most of them were riding side-by-side with a friend, or in larger groups of six or eight. The kids who were walking had not got this far down the road yet.

Some of the kids had their moms pick them up, but most of them rode their bikes or walked. Wingnut exclaimed that he's glad he takes the secret shortcut so he doesn't have to worry about always trying to avoid the Shulaks.

Suddenly Wingnut stopped dead in his tracks.

"Oh damn," he cursed, "Mom's going to kill me."

"What's the matter?" I demanded.

"I left my school bag under the bushes where we rested after running across the park. I took it off so I could lie down in the grass. Then the park caretaker came and we took off without it."

CHAPTER 4

When we arrived at Wingnut's house, we could see his mother through the window, standing in the kitchen doing her ironing. She glanced out every once in a while, but she did not appear to see us. The small path that led beside the house to the back door passed right under the window.

Wingnut tugged on my arm and led me around the other side of the house and through their broken-down, squeaky, old gate. I felt sure Wingnut's mom would hear the gate squeak and bang against the latch, but Wingnut didn't seem too concerned. I had already figured out that he planned to sneak into his house so his mom wouldn't notice that he didn't have his school bag with him. I wasn't sure exactly how he planned to do this, with his mom right there in the kitchen.

We arrived at his back door and he put his hand in the centre of the spot where the paint had worn off and gave the bottom a quick kick in the other worn spot. The door flew open and Wingnut boldly walked in and said,

"Come on, let's go to my room and I'll give you some comics." I thought for sure that his mom would be right there in the kitchen to greet us, as my mom would have, but we walked right past her as she continued her ironing. She never even looked around as the floor creaked and our loud footsteps disappeared up the hallway.

When we got to Wingnut's room he shut the door, reached under his bed, and pulled out a worn, crumpled cardboard box, lifted it up onto the bed and dumped out the contents. Rummaging through the pile, he selected an assortment of comics for me to take home.

I had enjoyed the stories from the first batch and I was excited to get some new adventures to read about. I told Wingnut that the operation payback story was my favorite; he agreed that it was also one of his favorites. We chatted for a while about some of the stories in the comics, and all the while, Wingnut was not looking too happy. I said,

"Perhaps it's time I went home, as Mom should be getting home soon."

"Well, my mom is home," he said, "and I wish she wasn't."

"Why do you say that?"

"Well, Mom gave me some money to pay for some library books that I lost, and she gave me strict instructions to bring home all the change, and the receipt from the library. Well, it's all in my school bag and now and I've lost that too. Mom's going to go berserk, when she finds out. I will probably get a good spanking with the fly swatter."

"Shall we go back and get it"? I asked. "It's probably still just lying in the grass, if no one has found it yet."

"Yeah," Wingnut said loudly and he grinned his big, whole-face grin. He said it so loudly that I looked toward the door, expecting Wingnut's mom to come bursting into the room at any second. He was quite excited and asked me to meet him by the wooden rail at the drain tunnel after dinner.

We had planned to tell our parents that we were going over to each other's houses to play. Then we would take the secret shortcut back to the park at the back of the school, retrieve Wingnut's school bag and be back home before anyone missed us. It sounded like a perfect plan.

I excitedly stuffed Wingnut's comics into my school bag, which was still strapped tightly to my back. We left his room and walked down the hall to the kitchen, where his mom was now folding the legs of her ironing table so that she could put it away in the closet. Once again, we walked right past her and she never turned around. I think my mom has eyes in the back of her head, as I couldn't even pull faces behind her back without her sensing it and spinning around just in time to catch me. But for some reason, Wingnut's mom was different.

We went out Wingnut's side gate, and as I reached the road I had a terrible feeling of dread.

I had ridden my bike to school that morning, and then run home by the shortcut. I had forgotten all about my bike, which I had left at school.

Then remembering our plan to retrieve the school bag, I was thrilled to realize that I would also be able to retrieve my bike at the same time.

I ate my dinner with a feeling of nervous apprehension, as I had never snuck out before, or told Mom that I was going to do something, only to do something else.

After dinner, I put on some old jeans, my gumboots and my favorite mucking-about shirt, told Mom I was going over to Wingnut's to play, and waited at the wooden rail at the side of the drain.

Wingnut appeared, wearing his same clothes and his turned-down gumboots. We climbed the rail with the barbed wire on it, jumped down the other side of the fence, and set off down the narrow track between the drain and the ditch, keeping a watchful eye on the ground for dead hedgehogs.

It was a warm evening. The breeze was swaying the trees and making waves of motion in the grass, and our shadows were long and dark and made monster-like images ahead of us, which seemed to flicker and dance as they passed over small bushes and clumps of grass.

Wingnut was walking in front of me, pointing out all the objects of interest that were floating or jammed up in small dams of junk, sticks, weed and garbage.

We found the dead hedgehog remains I had stepped in, splattered all over the track and the surrounding grass. It looked as though it had exploded when I stepped on it. We took a detour around it, wading through the long grass, which was up to our waists.

We were now on the edge of the small ditch that ran beside the drain. Wingnut looked down into the shallow water and stopped in his tracks.

"Look," he said, pointing into the ditch. As my eyes adjusted to the shadows that were cast over the ditch by the tall prickly hedge, I saw to my amazement something moving slowly in the water. Wingnut and I stood motionless for quite some time. There before us was a huge, black, shiny eel. It was eating the hedgehog guts off the stick that I had used to scrape off my shoes. It must have landed in the water when I flung it away earlier.

"Let's catch it," Wingnut whispered quietly, with a tone of excited enthusiasm.

"How are we going to do that?" I asked.

"We could get a long stick that has a Y-shaped forked end," he exclaimed, "and one of us could ram the stick down on it, and pin it to the bottom of the ditch, while the other jumps in and grabs it!"

"Yeah, that sounds like a great plan," I said. "I'll do the stick, and you can do the grabbing, because I'm sure not getting in there and grabbing that guts-eating thing. Anyway, they're too slimy to hold."

"Well, how about we get two sticks, one to pin it down with, and the other, we could make pointed, to spear it right through, so we can lift it out of the water!"

"OK," I said, as we rushed off excitedly in search of the perfect eel-catching sticks. We went quite a distance before we came upon an old tree which had a broken branch lying underneath it.

"Perfect!" Wingnut yelled, as we pounced upon the fallen branch and frantically tried to break off two of the dried branches. The wood was dry and hard and Wingnut cursed as he tried to break one off. It didn't budge.

"This one's perfect," he said, "but it won't break off."

"Let's both heave on it," I said, as we clasped our hands around the prized branch that was sticking straight up off the larger fallen branch. We heaved and pulled, it bent, and then sprung back so fast that we both lost our balance and fell down. We pulled again and again until finally it snapped off with a loud crack, like a gunshot. It was so sudden that we both fell in a heap in the grass, with the sticks still clasped in our hands.

"It's perfect! It splintered off into a knife point just the way I planned it," Wingnut chirped, and we both started to laugh as we picked ourselves up out of the long grass.

"Let's get a forked one." So without losing a moment, we snapped off two more until we ended up with a stout stick with a Y-shaped fork at the end. Carrying one each, we ran back to the spot where we had seen the eel. It was still there, eating guts.

Stalking quietly through the grass, we inched ourselves closer and closer to the edge of the ditch. The eel was in about five or six inches of water and was lying on the muddy bottom slowly moving its tail from side to side. It was a dark grey, muddy colour and it seemed to be very smooth and shiny. It was about as thick as a boy's arm and as long as his leg.

Wingnut was holding the pointed stick and I had the Y-shaped one.

"You go first," Wingnut whispered, "ram the stick down on it, just behind its head and push down hard. I'll spear it as soon as you have it pinned down."

"Then what?" I asked.

"Well, let's just catch it first," he replied, "then we can carry it home on the stick and we'll cook it up."

"Where are you going to tell your mom you got it from? My house?"

"We had better hurry up," Wingnut said, "before it swims away." He nudged me forward, and I crept closer and closer to the edge of the ditch. We were still fairly well hidden by the long grass, so crouching low, we stalked silently closer.

Now we could see the eel just below us. I raised the stick with two hands and moved it ever so slowly, down towards the water. Every muscle in my body was tensed; my eyes were fixed on the eel in the water. I could feel a light sweat forming on my forehead.

The eel hunt

"Do it now," Wingnut whispered.

With a grunt of effort, I rammed the stick down onto the eel with all my strength. The forks of the stick straddled it right behind the head. In an instant the eel exploded into a squirming, writhing, twisting frenzy. We both yelped with fright as the eel thrashed wildly in the water, turning it into a boiling mess of mud and weed.

Wingnut had his makeshift spear raised for action, but the water was now so muddy and churned-up he could not see his target, so he hurled the spear into the centre of the splashing. It pierced through the water, hardly making a splash and stuck there in the mud while the thrashing continued.

"Missed!" Wingnut yelled. He tried to pull the spear out of the mud but he could only just reach it with his outstretched fingertips. He quickly sat down in the grass, rolled up his boots and slid down the steep sides of the creek on his bum, his gumboots plopping into the water. As he stood up, the water was right up to the tops of his boots and the surrounding pressure had collapsed the tops of his boots to his legs.

He waded bravely towards the churning place where my stick was, grabbed his spear in both hands and heaved it from the mud. It was caked in black, gooey muck, which dripped off the end in large gobs. He shook the stick violently to get the muck off, causing a huge gob of mud to fly off and slap into my face. I winced as it splattered across my forehead and mouth. The shock of it made me jump, causing me to release the pressure on the stick. The eel instantly escaped and sped off up the creek, leaving a trail of mud and ripples.

"It's gone," Wingnut yelled, "let's go after it!" He turned his body to wade out of the creek but his feet didn't follow. He stood there windmilling his arms like he did the day he fell off the wall.

"My boots are stuck in the mud," he yelled. He was on the verge of falling over into the muddy water, so I reached out with my stick. He grabbed the end of it to steady himself and heaved on his right leg to try and free his boot. He grunted and groaned and screwed up his face as he heaved again.

Slowly, with a loud sucking sound, his boot came free. Standing on one leg, he took a huge step towards the bank, and leaning forward at a full stretch he pulled hard on his left leg. Suddenly the water gushed over the top of his boot, filling it instantly with cold water and mud. He pulled hard again and again, and then to his surprise his foot came free with such force that he was flung head-first into the grass where I was standing.

I grabbed his arm and pulled him up the side of the ditch. He lay in the grass, breathing heavily from his exertion.

"What happened?" he asked between breaths.

"You flicked a big gob of that muck into my face. That's what made me jump and let go of my stick." Wingnut began laughing heartily.

"It's not just on your face," he stammered. "You're covered in it." He found my mud-splattered appearance quite amusing, until he looked down and realized that his left boot was missing. His foot had come right out of it, and the gumboot was still stuck in the mud.

We prodded and probed for a long time, trying to find his boot, but it was covered by the mud and could not be seen.

"It's getting late," Wingnut declared. "We spent a lot of time trying to catch the eel; we had better go and get my school bag. Let's jam the spear into the ground here, to mark the spot, and I will come back in the weekend and try to find it."

So, with mud in our hair, on our clothes and faces, we set off once more down the track towards the school. Wingnut was leading the way, limping along with one boot and one squishy, muddy, floppy sock.

We trudged along the track in silence, peering down the grass-covered bank into the creek periodically, to see if we could see the eel that had escaped us.

Wingnut paused on the track after a while, to pull up his soggy sock. It was starting to dry out and small flakes of dried mud fell off, as he tried to pull it onto his foot so it wouldn't flop about when he walked. After two more sock-hoisting stops, we came to the bushes where we hoped Wingnut's school bag would be. Much to our relief, there it was lying face down in the flattened grass, where we had lain several hours earlier. It seemed like the events of the afternoon had happened some time ago instead of that very day.

Wingnut knelt down in the grass and picked up his school bag. It was coated in a fine layer of dust that had covered it when we crashed to the ground during the magpie attack.

"Look at that," Wingnut said, pointing to two sets of parallel marks scratched into the leather of his bag.

"Magpie claw marks," he declared. "It's a lucky thing I had my bag on my back to protect me from those."

"Oh!" I exclaimed. "How are we going to get across the park to get my bike? Your rotating magpie stick is broken, and we left the spear marking the spot where your gumboot is. There are no decent trees around here to get another stick from." We both slumped to the ground and lay on our backs, with our hands clasped behind our heads, to think about our predicament.

"I think we had better just wait here for a little while," Wingnut said after a long silence.

"The magpies will all be going to roost in their nests when the sun goes down, and then we can probably make it across the park without getting pecked and clawed to death."

We settled into comfortable positions to wait for the sun to go down. Wingnut was lying on his back with his head on his school bag, and I used a clump of grass as a pillow. It was a nice secluded spot under the bushes. The ground was sloping up behind us, creating a comfortable reclining position. The air was still fairly warm and a gentle breeze was rippling progressively through the trees, grass and bushes around us. We lay in companionable silence for quite some time, looking over the top of the grassy little hill on which we lay.

We could see across the expanse of the park before us. There were no people about, the shadows were long and slender and the whole scene looked mysterious and alien. Our thoughts were disturbed by the sound of a dog barking in the distance; we stirred and Wingnut sat up, looked around then flopped down again.

"Do you think we should get going?" I asked. "It's getting pretty dark and spooky-looking."

"Yeah, we might as well. I think the magpies are settling down now."

Setting off down the little hill, we ventured out into the open, cautiously peering upwards to check for attacking magpies.

I glanced at Wingnut, then clenched my fist and punched him hard on the arm.

"Where's your bag, you dummy? You've walked off and left it under the bushes again, after all we've been through, to get it!" Wingnut threw his arms in the air, thumped himself on the forehead, grinned his wide-faced grin and dashed back to our resting spot, threading his arms through the shoulder straps of his bag as he ran back to continue our uneventful crossing of the park.

My bike was right where I left it, except someone had knocked it over in their hurry to remove their own bike from the stand. Wheeling the bike out of the deserted schoolyard, we passed a building that had a wooden tower attached to the side of it. This tower housed the huge brass school bell, which was mounted on a shaft that pivoted in a greasy metal cradle. The shaft had a lever on the end, from which hung a long rope. Its end was tied to a metal knob, which prevented the bell from ringing in the wind.

"Hey, let's ring the bell," Wingnut yelled. He ran towards the tower, slipped the rope from its securing knob and gave it a hard yank. The bell swung easily, creating an almighty clang, as the knocker inside struck the side of the bell. The sound was startlingly crisp and clear in the quiet evening air.

Realizing that the sound could be heard for miles, and the nasty caretaker's house was just a short distance away, we took off at a run, with me pushing my bike and Wingnut running alongside.

Because we now had my bike and Wingnut had only one gumboot, we had no option but to ride the bike down the avenue, which ran across the front of the park. Wingnut sat side saddle on the cross bar of my bike, with his school bag banging on my chest each time I strained forward to pedal. We soon passed the park and the tennis courts and were now riding on the footpath in front of a long row of houses.

Some had white wooden fences, some had hedges, and some had stone walls, the same as Wingnut's house. We passed them one by one in a mesmerizing silence.

Smash! Something crashed into my front wheel, and exploded into a million pieces. The impact caused a dangerous wobble, nearly causing us to careen into the concrete sidewalk.

Smash again! There was another explosion of shattered stuff hitting the back wheel, and then another object smashed to bits on the sidewalk right in front of us. They seemed to be furiously crashing and exploding all around us. We were being bombarded by hard, dry clods of earth. Suddenly we spotted the attackers.

"It's the Shulaks!" Wingnut yelled. The two redheads were hiding behind the wall in front of their house with a bucket full of ammunition, gleefully hurling large clods of dirt at us as fast as they could. As I sped up to pass their house, Wingnut yelled at me to cross the road, to get out of range. I quickly glanced up and down the road for passing cars and, seeing none, I swerved out onto the road and sped across it to the other side.

There was a wide verge, which was covered with grass and huge oak trees. The soft grass slowed us down, and with Wingnut clutching the handlebars with both hands, it was very hard to ride and steer.

The Shulaks leaped over the wall, ran across the road and chased after us. I was pedaling as hard as I could but the Shulaks were gaining on us. Wingnut was rocking back and forth in an effort to urge our bike to go faster. The larger of the two red-haired brothers caught up to us, and at a full run, gave me an almighty hard shove, which sent us into an uncontrollable wobble.

We went crashing to the ground in a tangled heap of boys, bags and bike. The Shulaks were upon us in a flash, dancing around us, jeering, taunting and laughing at us both, while they threw the remaining dirt they had at us.

Wingnut had a trickle of blood running down the side of his face, which mixed into the dirt imbedded in his skin. His hair was littered with lumps of dirt and dust. He had been hit on the side of his face with one of the Shulaks' clods. Wingnut got to his feet and stood looking warily at the taunting bullies.

As I stood up, the bigger of the two pushed me hard. I stumbled, tripped on my bike, and fell heavily backwards on top of it. One of the protruding pedals stabbed me in the back as I fell. Wingnut came to my assistance, only to be shoved from behind and sent sprawling on top of me.

"How did you like that, goofy-looking, one-boot boy?"

"Can't your mommy afford to buy you two boots?" The smaller Shulak grabbed the end of Wingnut's floppy sock, which was dangling off the end of his foot. He ripped it off with a force that made Wingnut wince. The Shulak boy laughed and danced about, waving his trophy over his head, spun around three times and flung it high up into a nearby tree.

Wingnut swore at him using bad words that I had never heard before, but they sounded very appropriate. The Shulaks turned on Wingnut. They grabbed him, hauled him off the bike and me, pinned him to the ground, and wrestled the school bag off his back, dumping the contents onto the grass.

There was a half-eaten potato from Wingnut's lunch, some stumpy worn-out pencils, three homework books and two war comics. The Shulaks grabbed one of the comics each and threw the bag at Wingnut. He fended it off his face with his forearm and it spun end over end, tumbling into the grass.

The Shulaks heard a tinkling sound from the bag, so they raced over and snatched it up. The younger one searched through the bag. The older one snatched it from his brother, undid the small zipper that was inside the top flap, and thrust two of his fingers into the small zippered pocket, extracting all of Wingnut's mom's library money. He flashed the coins in the palm of his hand to his brother and they both laughed with glee at their find.

Wingnut looked on in horror as the Shulak plunged his coin-filled hand into his pants pocket, and the two bullies walked off towards the road.

They had walked some distance when Wingnut stooped to the ground and picked up a big clod of earth that had not been broken. He twisted his body, extended his arm back, and hurled the clod towards the Shulaks with all his might. We both stood and watched as the clod of dirt sped through the air, tumbling end over end, as it flew.

The Shulak brothers were now crossing the road, looking from side to side for approaching cars. The tumbling clod of dirt smashed into a million pieces, right in the middle of the big brother's back. He jumped straight up in the air with fright, startling his younger brother who thought they were about to be run over by a car.

In the next instant, the Shulaks realized what had happened. They spun around in the middle of the road and ran at full sprint towards us.

Wingnut scooped up his school bag and yelled,

"Run for it!"

We took off like two startled rabbits. We had a good head start on the Shulaks, even though Wingnut was hopping along in one gumboot.

When the enraged Shulaks reached the spot where my bike still lay on the ground, they suddenly gave up the chase and began to jump furiously on my bike, stamping and kicking with all their might.

Wingnut and I reached the safety of the first house past the park on that side of the road. We hid out of sight behind their fence.

After the Shulaks had wreaked their vengeance on my bike, they slowly wandered off in the direction of their house, behind the dingy grey stone wall.

When they were well out of sight, Wingnut and I glumly plodded over to the battle site, where he picked up the remains of his school bag contents. He hurled the leftover potato onto the road and put his pencils and books back into his bag.

I picked up my bike. The wheels were wobbly, the bell was broken off, and the handlebars were bent and crooked. We headed home in the dark, Wingnut holding the handlebars on one side of the bike, while I held the other. The wheels would not go around, so we lifted the front wheel off the ground and dragged the other all the way home like two pall bearers carrying a coffin, with Wingnut limping along with one bare foot.

We staggered past Wingnut's house in the near dark. He helped me stash the bike beside our garage, so my dad wouldn't see it until I had figured out what to do with it. Wingnut limped home in the dark by himself, not knowing what was going to happen when his mom learned he had lost his boot, his sock, and her library money.

It had been quite a day.

Chapter 5

The house was quiet when I woke in the morning. I lay in bed with the covers pulled up around my neck. My sheets and pillowcase still smelled nice and fresh from being hung outside on the clothesline, in the sun. My cat was curled up in a ball beside me, and the weight of him kept the covers on the bed tucked in tight behind me. The cat stirred and stood up as I tried to roll over. He came to my face, purring and nuzzling up to me, nudging his head up and down and forcing himself in under the covers, slinking his way down into the warmth of the bed before curling up with his head on my hip.

We both dozed quietly, until I realized that I had better get up, as my tummy was starting to gurgle to let me know that I needed to go to the toilet. I wasn't really ready to get up just yet, so I lay there for a little while. My tummy gave another gurgle and quite unexpectedly, I let go a long steady fart.

Not one of those popping ones, or even a loud one, just a silent fizzer. The cat let out a frantic meow and started to struggle about under the covers, trying to escape. I kept the blankets pulled up tightly under my chin, until the smell went away. The cat was becoming quite desperate, and was beginning to use his claws to escape.

I threw back the covers and the cat sprang out in an instant, and made a dash for the door as I made a dash for the bathroom.

Later that morning, I thought I had better tidy my room, as Mom had asked me several times and I felt that perhaps her patience might be wearing a little thin. My brother had gone to a friend's house for the whole week so I had the whole room to myself. His stuff was strewn all over the place, so I kicked it all clear of my side and began picking up clothes and putting toys away.

I unearthed the latest war comics that Wingnut had lent me. I opened one and flopped down on my bed, and soon became immersed in reading it. It was another great story, and I didn't stop until I had read the entire thing. Suddenly Mom came into the room and saw me lying on the bed reading my comic.

"Well, young man," she said, "I thought you were going to tidy up this pig sty of a room, instead of lounging around reading comics."

"I was tidying my room!" I declared.

"Oh, it sure looks like it." Mom said. When she left, I stashed my comics away and cleaned up my room, which looked pretty good, I thought.

I found ten dollars under my bedside lamp, that my grandmother had given me. It was still folded in half, inside the birthday card. I took it out and put it into my shirt pocket. After breakfast I did the rest of my chores, which takes me quite a while, as I have to cut a box full of kindling wood to light the fire in the living room in the evening. Now that the hot weather has come, I don't have to do that anymore, but I do have to clean and polish all the shoes. There are usually about seven pairs lined up waiting for me.

Saturday always seems to be a day to just mess about and see what happens. I finished all my chores and went outside to get my bike. I was nearly to the garage when I realized that my trusty bike had been stashed amongst the assorted "come in handy one day" junk that was jammed in between the fence and the side of the garage. I slipped quietly around to the back of the garage and parted the shrubs that concealed the hiding place of my poor, mangled bike.

It was more badly damaged than I had realized when we had dragged it home the night before.

I was planning to ride my bike to the little grocery store at the end of the street, to buy an ice cream and perhaps some chocolate with my birthday money. I told Mom I was going. I didn't want her to see me walking down the driveway, because she would surely want to know why I was walking, instead of riding my bike. I knew I'd be in big trouble when Mom or Dad saw it. I decided that I would try to fix it up a bit and maybe they wouldn't notice.

In the meantime, my mind was fixed on ice cream and chocolate. I squeezed sideways through the hedge and headed through the long grass in the vacant lot next door. It wasn't entirely vacant, as there was an old hermit man whom we never spoke to living in a rickety little hut of a cottage, which was set a long ways back off the road.

My mom had told us all, several times, that we were not to visit old Mac's cottage alone. We were definitely forbidden to go inside the house with him.

I threaded my way through the long grass that was still cold and wet with the morning dew. The early sunlight was sparkling on the spider webs that were woven between the tall stalks of grass that had matured and gone to seed. I broke off one of those stalks and used it like a wand, to magically wave away the spider webs as I walked, so I didn't get them stuck on my face.

Reaching the road, I walked up the slight slope that formed over the tunnel, where the drain ran under the road. I peered over the wooden top rail of the fence which had the barbed wire on it, and surveyed the scene of water flowing out the end of the tunnel, on its way to the estuary, carrying with it its assortment of scungy rubbish.

It was very quiet except for a few birds singing, and a dog barking in the distance. I could hear the creepy, gurgling sound coming from within the dark depths of the tunnel. It gave me a cold shudder. I pulled back from the fence and walked to the end of the street, where I took the little narrow path that was worn through the grass by all the people taking a shortcut to the grocery store.

I bought a double scoop of ice cream, and four chocolate fish made of soft marshmallow, coated with chocolate. They were supposed to be shaped like fish. I thought they didn't actually look anything like fish, but they sure tasted good—in fact, I loved them!

I had the chocolate fish in a small white paper bag in one hand, and my huge ice cream in the other. The day had warmed up a lot now and I had to keep turning the ice cream around and around, and lick it continuously as it rotated, to prevent it from melting all over my hand. I pretty well had it under control as I reached my street.

A slight movement caught my eye, and I looked across the street towards the church on the corner, next to Wingnut's house. There, on the front steps of the church, sat Wingnut all by himself with his head in his hands.

I crossed the street and sat quietly beside him. He sensed my presence, slowly looked up, and tried to pretend that he wasn't crying. I didn't speak as I handed him my ice cream. He wiped his eyes with the back of his hand, sniffed twice, and broke the sad face with his big, ear-to-ear grin.

We took turns sharing the ice cream until it was all gone, without talking.

We wiped our sticky hands on our pants and our sticky faces on our sleeves.

"Why are you sitting here by yourself?" I asked.

"I'm in deep trouble when Mom finds out that I've lost one of my gumboots, my sock, and all the money for the library books."

"Yeah, I'll be in deep trouble too, when Dad finds out that my bike is wrecked."

"What are we going to do?" Wingnut whined.

"How much money did the Shulaks take from your bag?"

"Six dollars," Wingnut said glumly.

"Six dollars!" I declared. "I have six dollars right here in my pocket—it's my own money that I got for my birthday. I'll give it to you to pay back your mom."

"Ha! I've got a plan," Wingnut exclaimed gleefully.

"Your wonderful plans got us into this mess in the first place."

"No, no!" Wingnut said excitedly. "If you lend me the money, I'll go home and put it into my school bag like nothing happened. Then we'll go down the secret shortcut and fish out my boot. Then we can go to your house and I'll help you fix your bike."

"Let's go!" Wingnut yelled, as we ran off at top speed to his house, dashed around the side path, where he kicked the gate open with a crash, kicked open his back door, and boldly marched inside to his room. He reached under his bed, pulled out his school bag, placed the money in the zippered pocket, wiped off all the dust and mud, and slid it back under his bed.

"Ok, let's go get my boot," he said excitedly as we dashed from his room.

As we reached the kitchen, Wingnut's mom walked around from the other room, carrying a basket of clean laundry in front of her. She let out a horrible squawk as she dropped the basket in fright, and began barking like a seal and making really freaky noises at us. I ran out the back door as fast as I could, but Wingnut stopped where he was and as I looked back, his mother and he were frantically waving their arms about and wiggling their fingers at each other. Suddenly his mom stopped, smiled, and Wingnut spun around and ran to catch up to me.

We ran non-stop all the way to the bridge that crossed the drain. We climbed over the wooden rail and headed off down the little track through the long grass between the concrete drain and the ditch. We soon reached the spot where I had stepped on the dead, rotting hedgehog. The squashed remains were still there, crawling with flies and hundreds more white maggots, wiggling and squirming all through it.

"I dare you to step in it again," Wingnut challenged.

"Step in it yourself, one-boot boy." We both laughed and headed for the stick that marked the spot where Wingnut's boot lay buried. He suddenly put a finger to his lips to signal me to be quiet. We stalked silently through the grass to the edge of the creek, and peered into the water very carefully, in case the eel had returned.

The mud had settled and the water was now clear. There, in the middle of the creek, was a round ring in the mud, formed by the top of Wingnut's gumboot.

I held the end of the marker stick, as Wingnut slid barefoot in his short pants, down the bank of the creek. He immediately sank into the mud up to his knees. He reached his hand down into the mud, got his fingers under the boot with one hand, gripped the top with the other, and easily lifted the waterlogged boot from the mud. He poured out all the water and swished the boot around several times to wash it.

"Good as new," he declared with a grin. He walked barefoot down the track, holding his boot upside down, swinging it as he walked, to drain and dry it.

As we reached the dark, gurgling tunnel, Wingnut lay on his stomach with his head and shoulders over the edge of the drain, and strained himself to look into the darkness of the tunnel.

"Hey, I can see daylight at the other end," he yelled, with his voice echoing eerily through the tunnel. Standing up, he said,

"I dare you to walk through there," challenging me with a menacing scowl on his face.

"That's creepier than the dead hedgehog dare," I stammered.

"I'll do it if you will," he said, challenging me again.

"I'll tell you what! I'll go home and get my other gumboot and a hat, and you go home, get your gumboots and a hat, and I'll meet you right here in fifteen minutes."

"What do we need a hat for?" I asked nervously.

"Well, when I looked through, I saw big spider webs across the entrance, and a hat would stop the spiders from getting into our hair."

We sped off in opposite directions to our houses, to fetch our boots and hats. I also found an old painting shirt and a pair of old gloves. I bundled them up under my arm and ran back to join Wingnut at the tunnel. He appeared with both of his boots rolled up, carrying an old, wide-brimmed straw gardening hat and a scarf. We climbed the fence once more, and sat on the edge of the drain and ate the chocolate fish, which were by now really melted and gooey.

Wingnut put his pants over the top of his boots, wrapped the scarf several times around his neck, and jammed his hat tight on his head.

I put on my hat, and put the painting shirt over my head, with the neck of the shirt around my face. I tied the shirt arms under my chin, and the tail of the shirt was covering my neck and back. Wingnut saw me putting on my gloves, and pulled his hands up inside his sleeves and held the cuffs with his fingers.

We looked at each other and burst out laughing. Wingnut strutted up and down and did some sexy turns like a fashion model.

He thought he was extremely funny. Our smiles faded rapidly as we climbed down the concrete sides of the drain. The toes of our gumboots probed for the ends of the pipes that protruded into the sides, which served as footholds.

Spider adventure

We stood in silence in the water, with the current flowing around our boots, as we peered nervously into the black hole before us.

The eerie, gurgling sound seemed much louder now that we were right there in the water. The top of the tunnel was low, and we had to duck down and walk stooped-over to prevent scraping the top of the tunnel with our hats. We cautiously stepped into the darkness side by side. We had only taken about ten steps into the dark, damp, lightless tunnel when thoughts of trolls and escaped convicts flashed through my mind. I could feel the tingle of fear on the back of my neck. I felt it again.

"Ahh! There's something on my neck!" I screamed. I turned a little to let Wingnut take a look. He squinted in the darkness, lifting up the brim of his hat so he could see. Then he screamed, scaring mc half to death.

"Spiders!" he squealed.

"You're absolutely covered with huge spiders; your hat's thick with their webs." I looked around white-faced.

"And so are you," I croaked in a panic-stricken voice.

"Let's get out of here." We thrashed about on the spot, trying to turn around, but each time we tried to turn around or walk backwards, our hats hung up on the ceiling of the tunnel, which was seething with black spiders. They were dropping into the water all around us.

"Let's keep going forward," Wingnut said with authority.

"The spiders are only on our clothes. Bend over low so that your hat doesn't scrape them off the ceiling and keep walking." I was in a cold sweat, but Wingnut moved forward so I did the same. We could feel the endless tug of the thousands of spider webs that were laced through the entire length of the tunnel, pulling on our hats as we pushed through them. We could make out the shapes of the huge spiders that raced out of their hiding places as they felt the slight pressure on their webs.

We were now about halfway through the tunnel, and we could hear the creepy, gurgling sound, loud and clear. I was convinced that it was a troll hiding in there, gurgling with delight at the sight of the two tasty boys he would rip apart with his bare hands, and whose arms and legs he would chew the flesh off with his crooked, razor-sharp, yellow teeth. He would eat us, spiders and all.

Wingnut slipped, stumbled, and nearly fell into the murky water. He shouted,

"Be careful! There's something in the water down there."

I froze on the spot and looked at him with terror-stricken, popping eyes.

"There's something smooth and slimy," he wailed. I remained motionless with my eyes fixed on the spot at my feet. The water seemed to be very smooth. It formed a rounded bulge, which glistened in the little bit of web-filtered daylight that was coming in from the far end of the tunnel. I gingerly jabbed it with my foot then jumped back—nothing happened. I touched it again, then again, and still nothing happened.

"It's a pipe," I said. "It's only a pipe crossing the flow of water. That's what makes the gurgling sound in here—it's the water flowing over this pipe."

"Phew!" Wingnut sighed.

"I'm sure glad of that, I thought we were goners for sure—I thought it was a giant eel lying there."

"I thought it was a troll."

"Let's get out of here."

When we reached the far end of the tunnel, it was a huge relief to finally stand up straight. As we looked at each other in the daylight, we were horrified to see a thick coating of spider webs, and hundreds of spiders all over our clothes. We clambered up the sides of the drain and frantically danced about, shedding our clothes and flicking the spiders off into the grass as we did so.

We stripped to the waist and examined each other for spiders. We dragged our old, spider web-covered clothes and hats around in the grass, and were able to rub off most of the webs.

I placed all my old clothes into the shirt that I had spread out on the ground and tied them all up in a bundle by folding the shirt up around them and tying the sleeves together. Wingnut scrunched all his old clothes into his hat, and tucked the bundle under his arm and marched off along the narrow bank of the drain.

We were now on the opposite side of the road. We had never been down this side of the drain before.

The little ditch that we had followed in the direction of our school was not on this side of the road for some reason. There was just a narrow strip of grass bordered by the drain on the left, and a high prickly hedge on the right.

"Hey, where are you going now?" I yelled.

"We're going to your house to fix your bike," Wingnut replied without turning around. I ran to catch up with him.

"Well, we had better climb the fence and walk down the road. That's the way to my house."

"We can get to your house this way," Wingnut stated confidently.

We passed under a large pussy willow tree, laden with large yellow blossoms.

"That looks like a great treehouse tree," Wingnut stated. I looked up at the tree, which was thick with green leaves, and had many branches, which splayed out from the thick trunk.

"Yeah," I agreed. "It would be great for a treehouse. Nobody would even know it was there with all those leaves on it."

As we reached the edge of old Mac's property, we veered left and walked along the side of the little hedge, that was really nothing more than a row of small poplar trees that grew along the border of my dad's property. We squeezed through a gap in the trees, and found ourselves at the back of our garage. We were totally out of sight from my mom's kitchen window. We threw our spider clothes down on the small patch of lawn that was at the back of the garage, and proceeded to extract my bike from the pile of stuff beside the garage. We dragged it out into the open and I leaned it against the little apricot tree that grew in the middle of the patch of lawn. I never came to this part of our property, as it was tucked away behind the garage, and it seemed to be a damp, shady spot. Anyway, it was a great spot to prop up my busted bike, to assess the damage, without being detected.

Wingnut tugged and wiggled at various parts of the bike and asked if I could get some tools to start working on it. I had lots of tools in my garage. I don't know exactly where they all came from, but they have been there for as long as I can remember.

I had a little tool bag that was loaded with tools for bikes. They were funny looking things, but there were things that fitted on every nut and bolt on a bike. We found a piece of pipe beside the garage and we managed to use it to straighten up the handlebars. We pried a few other things back into shape, and had soon straightened nearly everything except the wobbly wheel.

"My brother's a genius with things like this," I told Wingnut. "I'll ask him to help us when he comes home. I bet he'll be able to fix it." Wingnut paused thoughtfully, then I noticed his big, wide-faced grin beginning to appear on his face.

I stared at him for a few moments, wondering what was brewing inside his busy mind.

"I know where there is a whole pile of old bikes. I bet we could find a straight wheel to fit your bike."

"Yeah, right!" I said. "Where do you ever find a pile of bikes just lying around?"

"There's not only bikes—there's all sorts of neat junk. Piles and piles of stuff that people have thrown away—it's an awesome little garbage dump. I found it one day when I was walking down the secret shortcut. I heard a noise in the grass on the other side of the drain, and it scared me actually, because I could hear this rustling sound in the grass, but I couldn't see what it was.

"I froze on the spot and watched, prepared to make a run for it if something came after me.

"After a while I saw that it was a chicken nesting in the grass there. The mother hen had five little chicks and she was scratching in the grass, exposing stuff for the chicks to peck at. I thought my mom would be pleased if I could catch the hen and her chicks and take them home with me. We could have free eggs every day.

"I walked along the side of the drain for a short distance, to a place where the ground was flat between the little ditch and the drain. When I found a good spot, I walked back and forth crossways to the track, and flattened all the grass to make a runway so I could get a good run up, to jump the drain. I made the best jump ever, but I did fall into a patch of thistles on the other side when I landed.

"Anyway, I crouched down in the grass and snuck up on the chicken, but she heard me coming and ran off in fright through a gap in the prickly hedge, so I followed her. She was trotting along with all the chicks following behind. There was a huge, open area behind the hedge that I had never seen. It was full of massive piles of dirt and big holes in the ground that were full of water. It was just like pictures of the bomb craters that I saw in my war comics.

"Off in the distance I saw a bright flash of light that was going on and off, so I squatted down in the grass and watched it for a while. The light was really bright, and was shining right at me. It was blindingly bright, and after watching it for a while, I realized that it might be the sun reflecting off something. So I snuck up on the source of light and found that it was a broken mirror jutting out from a pile of junk. It was flashing because there was a dirty old piece of black plastic flapping in the wind in front of it.

"Anyway, this place was awesome. It was way out in the middle of this huge area and people had dumped tons of stuff into the big hole that was there. That's where I saw all the bikes thrown in a heap. Let's go and see if we can find you a new wheel. Bring your tool bag and let's go."

CHAPTER 6

Excitedly, we stashed the bike and all the stuff that we had strewn about, back into the narrow area beside the garage, then we slipped back through the poplar hedge and ran through our newfound shortcut across the front of old Mac's house. Once we were on the track alongside the drain, we relaxed a bit and checked the small ditch for eels once in a while.

We soon reached the spot where Wingnut said he had flattened the grass for his run up to jump the drain. It took no time at all for us to stomp the grass down and declare the area free from trip hazards.

"You go first," I said to Wingnut once we were ready to make the jump.

"No, you go first!" Wingnut said. We were both scared of making the jump because the concrete side of the drain was a little intimidating, to say the least.

"You've already jumped it once, you go first."

"OK, I'll show you how it's done," he said.

Backing down our flattened grass runway, all the way to the ditch, Wingnut maximized his distance. He took a sprinter's starting stance, plucked up his courage, and sprang off at top speed toward the near edge of the drain. Launching himself off the edge, he soared through the air with his arms and legs stretched forward. The tops of his rubber gumboots were flapping in the rush of air that passed him. He landed safely on the other side, but as his feet hit the ground, his forward momentum pivoted him over his feet and he sprawled face first into all the lush growth that was blanketing the far bank of the drain. He emerged from the grass and weeds wearing a huge, victorious grin.

"Your turn!" he yelled.

I backed up just as Wingnut had done. Encouraged by his success, I made a flying leap for the other side, barely making the distance. The heel of my boot caught the concrete edge of the drain and threw me off balance. I quickly twirled myself around to prevent falling backwards into the mucky water in the bottom of the drain. I jabbed my other foot at the ground to catch my balance, but my foot just missed the concrete edge. The inside of my bare leg grated against the concrete, from my knee to my bum. I seized up from the shock and the pain and fell over backwards into the drain.

Wingnut rushed to the edge and peered down to see me sprawled on my back in the dirty shallow water.

"Get up." he yelled, as he stretched out his hand to pull me up the side. With his help, I scrambled out of the drain, dripping wet with smelly water that stung like mad, and examined my injuries. I had multitudes of bright red scratches and grazes all the way up the inside of my right leg. In places there were deeper cuts where the blood had already begun to well up and trickle down my leg.

"Crikey! I bet that stings," Wingnut chirped unsympathetically. "It's a good thing I brought my hankie today. Do you have one?"

"Yes," I replied sulkily.

"Well, let's bandage your leg with them." Wingnut flicked his handkerchief a few times in an effort to remove the pocket fluff and bits of leftover dried snot that was smeared on it here and there. I did the same, and we soon had the two hankies tied around the worst spots on my stinging leg. I wrung out my shirt and shook off the scummy stuff from the water that had stuck to it, and put it back on. I left it unbuttoned so it could dry in the breeze.

We headed off through the grass, with Wingnut leading the way, and me limping along behind, towards Wingnut's wondrous garbage dump.

The blood had dried by the time we arrived at the dump, and the hankies were now stuck to my skin, pulling a little painfully with each step.

Wingnut's description turned out to be quite accurate. There was all kinds of stuff there.

The hole he had described was much bigger than I had imagined. It was a huge depression, surrounded by all the dirt that had been excavated from it years ago. The hills of dirt had very steep sides and were densely overgrown with grass, weeds and thistles.

Wingnut had skidded his way down the steep side of the hill on which I stood, and was darting about all over the place, gleefully checking out all the assorted junk as he came to it. There were old fridges, steel drums, stoves, car bodies, broken chairs, doors, tyres, bits of wood and metal strewn everywhere, old, rotten mattresses, bundles of rusty fencing wire, and of course discarded bikes of all sizes and shapes.

"Here's a good one," Wingnut shouted excitedly, so I hobbled down the hill to help him untangle the bike from the pile of junk which half buried it. It looked like the wheels were the same size as mine, so Wingnut and I set about hauling all the junk aside, to free the half-buried bike from its tangled resting place.

"Let's carry it over there," said Wingnut, grabbing hold of the handlebars and finally wrenching it free.

"We can work on it on top of that pile of old wood."

"Good idea," I agreed, and between us, we carried it across the treacherous mass of broken glass, splintered wood and protruding metal spikes.

Once on the woodpile, a quick trial and error exercise soon revealed the right tool with which to undo the wheel nuts, and with a few frantic jiggles, the front wheel of the bike came free. I held on to it while Wingnut lifted the rest of the old bike above his head and stomped around, grunting and growling like King Kong, as he hurled it with all his might across the junk pile. It landed upside down, crashing into an old window frame that still had glass in it. The glass shattered with the loud, satisfying tinkling sound that only breaking glass can make. Wingnut was heading out across the sea of rubble, leaping and bounding from pile to pile, towards the spot where the bike had landed.

"Hey, come take a look at this," he shouted.

I left the wheel and the tools on the wood pile and walked gingerly in Wingnut's direction. It was quite difficult not to flex my leg too much as the piles of junk were very uneven and unsteady. The dried blood on the hankie bandage pulled painfully on my cuts as I clambered slowly to see what Wingnut had discovered. When I finally reached the spot, Wingnut was busy standing old window frames up and propping them in a row, so that they would support each other in an upright position.

"What on earth are you doing now?" I asked, as he ripped yet another frame from the tangled pile.

"Look at all these cool windows—there's dozens of them." As my eyes scanned the scene, I realized that we were standing on top of a huge pile of glass windows, many of which were still in their frames and unbroken. I helped Wingnut in his quest to stand up about ten of the old windows, all in a row.

"There, that will do," he muttered, as he checked them to ensure that they were all secure in their upright positions. We retreated back over the tangled mess to the safety of the hill that surrounded the junk pit. From this elevated position, we could see all the windows that Wingnut had erected, in a long wall, about the width of a road away from us. It soon became clear what Wingnut's intentions for the windows were, as he began to gather a sizeable pile of egg-sized stones from the ground beneath his feet.

I frantically began doing the same, with a building sense of excitement. Suddenly we stopped gathering, and stood looking at each other in an uncomfortable silence. Neither of us spoke for a minute or two.

"I'm going first!" I yelled at Wingnut.

"It was my idea. I'm first," he retorted bluntly. We were both getting angry, thinking that the other was going to have the advantage with the limited targets. Wingnut's case that the whole thing was his idea, won the argument. Having won, he softened his position and compromised with the generous gesture of us both starting at the same time.

We braced ourselves, with our feet planted firmly apart, and with our respective piles of stones between our feet. We both had our left legs forward, towards the wall of standing windows, and four choice stones in each hand. We were poised like cats about to pounce.

"One, two, three, fire!" Wingnut yelled. We wasted no time setting our aim. We just hurled the stones one by one at the glass windows as fast as we could throw them. My first throw went high, and Wingnut's went wide, but we soon settled down into some serious stone throwing. The sound of the almighty smash as a stone hit its target, and the resulting tinkling of the broken glass cascading down in millions of shattered bits, stirred up a primitive war-like instinct to destroy. We hurled stone after stone as hard and fast as we could pick them up off the ground. It was a frenzy of destruction that little boys and girls almost never get to satisfy, but this day we were free to smash at will, and we did.

Eventually we tired, and returned to the woodpile to retrieve our wheel and the tool bag. Tucking the wheel under one arm and the bag under the other, we once again made the perilous trip across the tangled mess. Our eyes couldn't help scanning the intriguing assortment under our feet. Even off in the distance things of interest distractingly caught our eyes.

I was focused on getting the wheel and myself to the safety of the hilltop at the edge of the pit, as it was painful to be hopping and jumping from place to place in search of secure footing.

Wingnut, on the other hand, was wrestling some newfound treasure from one of the piles. I didn't look back at him until I reached the top of the hill. He had found the remains of an old baby carriage that still had four good wheels on it. He dragged it from its resting place over to the woodpile, which we had used as the wheel removal place. He was sorting through a variety of shattered boards, and finally settled on one in particular. He was grinning from ear to ear as he used a piece of metal that he had found to hammer the board into place on the baby carriage frame. There were lots of nails sticking up everywhere. He found a few that were loose enough to pull out with his fingers, so he straightened them with his piece of metal, then nailed them through the frame and bent the protruding ends over with a few well-placed hits.

He had soon completed his creation and dragged it over the junk, and placed it in front of me at the top of the hill.

"How's that?" he crowed. He had made a really fine go-cart with a little wooden seat, placed directly over the back axle.

Wingnut walked purposefully across the top of the hill and headed down the steep incline on the other side. He was keeping his feet together, shuffling them rapidly to form a track down the hill, to flatten the grass. I did the same behind him, to enhance the effect. After three or four trips up and down the hill, we had soon flattened out a fairly decent track down which we could run Wingnut's go-cart. Wingnut turned to face me as we stood at the top of the hill, looking down the track we had created. He wore a serious expression, as he said in a stern, matter of fact manner,

"I'm definitely going first this time—not only was it my idea, I built it."

"OK, OK," I said in agreement, as Wingnut carefully lined up the go-cart with the centre of the track. He placed his feet on the front axle and sat himself down on the board that he had nailed across the back axle.

Go-cart

He sat motionless for a minute, psyching himself up. He rocked back and forth a few times and the go-cart began to roll forward slowly. As all four wheels went over the edge, it rapidly picked up tremendous speed. Before it was even half way down the hill it was bouncing, bumping and swerving dangerously. I could see Wingnut being bounced so hard his backside was pounding down on the board seat. He was going so fast his hair was blown back over his head, his shirt was flapping furiously, and he was screaming at the top of his lungs. It was like watching a movie scene in slow motion, as Wingnut was being pounded about, barely able to hold on.

Suddenly, Wingnut appeared to be jumping about more than what was caused by the violent action of the speeding go-cart. He was shifting his weight about so frantically that he finally caused the go-cart to veer abruptly to the left, roll over, and spill him into a tumbling tangle of go-cart and flailing arms and legs.

The go-cart finally came to rest upside down on Wingnut's chest. He leaped up in a flash and was dancing about like an Indian doing a war dance, still screaming at the top of his lungs.

"What's the matter?" I yelled.

"Are you OK?"

"No, I am not OK," he screamed at the top of his lungs. "One of the nails that I bent over came loose, and the nail speared me in the bum about forty times on the way down the damn hill." I paused in shock for a moment at the thought.

"Crikey that must sting a bit!" I yelled from the top of the hill.

I hobbled slowly down the grassy slope, nursing my cuts and grazes, to help Wingnut. By the time I reached the bottom, he already had blood seeping through his punctured pants. He was looking very pale, as he staggered around trying to shake off the pain. Since my bleeding had stopped, and his had only started, I untied the crusty handkerchief that Wingnut had donated to me, folded it into a tidy square, and offered it back to him.

He gingerly placed it down the back of his underpants, in an attempt to bandage his punctured and bleeding bum cheek. We left the go-cart in the grass where it lay, and the two of us limped off forlornly, retracing our steps, like a couple of defeated, wounded soldiers. Our only spoil of war was one used bike wheel, which I had tucked under my arm.

CHAPTER 7

I was so hungry at dinnertime I ate everything on my plate. Mom asked me what I did today.

"I played with Wingnut," I said.

She asked me what happened to my leg. I paused for a moment before I answered. A lot of things had changed recently, since I met Wingnut. First, I had lied about going to Wingnut's house, and now I can't possibly tell her everything we did today. She wouldn't understand what great fun it was smashing all those windows. She wouldn't understand that I nearly made it, when Wingnut and I jumped the drain.

"I slipped off the wall in front of Wingnut's house today, and grazed my leg, but it's better now," I said. My heart was racing and I felt a cold sweat creep up my chest and spread all over my face. My mom always knew when I was lying, and getting found out was the worst thing ever.

There was a creepy, long silence at the dinner table. I sat there staring at my plate. I knew I would have to confess the whole day's activities, and I would be forbidden to go down by the drain, or to the dump again, and the penalties would be considerable. I could feel my heart pounding in my chest. I could hear the pulse of the veins in my neck, echoing in my ears.

Mom slid her chair back with a loud shuddering sound. She stood up slowly and walked around the table towards me. Time stood still. The seconds ticked over slowly, keeping rhythm with my pounding pulse, as she got closer and closer to where I sat. She came up behind me and clasped two powerful hands on the back of my chair and skidded it, with me still motionless on it, around to face her. I realized that I was holding my breath in terror. She leaned over and examined my scratches and grazes. When she finally spoke, I nearly jumped out of my skin.

"You had better put some antiseptic in your bath tonight. You don't want to get an infection."

My relief was indescribable. I cleared off the entire table by myself and scraped all the plates, and stacked them next to the sink for washing. I took the tablecloth off, and went outside and shook it like a victorious bullfighter.

The hot bath water stung the cuts as much as getting them in the first place, but I must admit my leg felt much better once I got it cleaned up. I put some bandages on the worst bits, and went to bed.

My sleep was full of ditches, junk, bike wheels, blood, broken glass and spiders.

Mom woke me in the morning by telling me that it was time to get up for church. I moaned and groaned and pretended to be so sleepy that I just couldn't rouse myself. Then to my utter astonishment, Mom said,

"I don't think you will miss much if you don't go to church today, why don't you have a sleep in instead, and we will be home in two hours."

I was speechless with disbelief. Every Sunday of our lives, my brother, sister and I were dragged, protesting, from our beds to attend Sunday school, rain or shine. Now, all of a sudden, I don't have to go if I don't want to; I can actually sleep in?

"Is this a trick?" I asked.

"No," Mom said, "the Sunday school teacher is sick today, so it's cancelled until she gets better. Bye! We'll see you when we get home."

"Wow!"

I lay in bed on my back, with my hands clasped behind my head. My cat walked silently into my room and jumped lightly up onto the bed. He padded around in a circle three times and flopped himself down by my hip. It was very quiet; there was no noise from inside the house. The only sound I could hear was a church bell ringing in the distance, calling all the faithful to church, and the faint noise of a dog barking far away.

The morning sunlight was making an angel glow in my room, and the curtains on my window were slowly pulsing in and out in the weak breeze, as if they were breathing. My thoughts drifted from one of the previous day's events to another: there were magpies, eels, spiders, and broken glass, but the most significant of all was the thought that all the things that happened yesterday were caused as a result of being attacked by the Shulaks and the damage that they inflicted on my bike, not to mention the loss of Wingnut's library money. My thoughts drifted aimlessly from one event to another. It was so quiet in the house; there was no distraction from the thoughts in my head and the images in my mind's eye.

I began to visualize the new wheel that we had brought home from the dump, and all the things that had happened since we left to find it. I daydreamed about putting on the new wheel and working to straighten out all of the bent parts. It reminded me of Wingnut's war comic and the soldiers working on the broken-down army truck, to ready it as a decoy.

"That's it. That's what I'll do with my bike." I sat bolt upright in my bed. The cat startled and leaped off in one bound, and ran out the door.

"It's time for Operation Payback!"

I threw back the sheets on my bed, pulled on my clothes, and walked quickly into the kitchen to make some toast. I was feeling very excited about the idea, and I wanted to tell Wingnut right away. I ate the small breakfast and excitedly headed off through the poplar hedge, crossed through the new shortcut trail that led in front of old Mac's house, and ended up on the road to Wingnut's house.

The street was very quiet; there were no people about, and no cars on the road. I soon realized that I was walking up the gentle slope that led up and over the bridge across the drain. I looked to my left across the road, and I could see all the way down the narrow track that ran down beside the drain, and the little ditch on the other side. The grass was now flattened out a little more than it was the first time I went down there, as Wingnut and I had made several trips down his secret shortcut since then. As I reached the top of the bridge, I looked to my right. On that side, I could see the drain disappearing into the distance. There was a narrow bank on the right side of it, with a very narrow track leading through the long grass, which must have been made years ago.

I tried to see how far it went, but it simply disappeared from view into the mass of grass through which it led. I remembered Wingnut telling me that the drain led all the way to the sea on that side, and ended at the old wooden floodgates. I had no idea what might be down there in that direction; it was as mysterious and unknown as a long road to China, or setting off across the ocean in a raft, having only the wind blowing you wherever it chooses, and to whatever fate it decides. I paused at the top of the bridge and looked down into the shallow water below. It was flowing silently out the end of the tunnel, and since it was so quiet, I could hear the spooky gurgling sound and I felt a shiver tingle up my back, as I remembered our very freaky spider adventure.

CHAPTER 8

I could hear a radio playing through a window as I walked past someone's house. It sounded like the babbling of a sports announcer as he was trying to make a dull game seem like the most exciting event ever.

I crossed the street and was now on the same side as Wingnut's house. It was cool, dark and shady on this side of the street, as the old houses that were on this side had large trees growing around them, which made their properties seem spooky and dark. The second house in the row had the thickest, droopiest trees of them all.

I casually peered into a small opening that had been created by a tree that had died years ago. I could see that the lawn did not grow very well under these thick trees and the ground was dark, damp, and smelly. There was an assortment of old stuff piled up against the side of the house. An old wooden ladder caught my eye. The top of it was leaning against the wall at a shallow angle and the bottom was placed on the outside of the collection of old stuff that was stored there. As

I looked away, a faint flash of colour caught my attention. Red. A glimpse of red. It was so dark and shady there beside the house, I squinted my eyes, straining to see. I walked into the trees for a closer look, and without planning to, I found myself completely through the trees, standing at the foot of the old ladder, right on these people's property. I had the urge to run back into the daylight, but it was quiet, and I was sure that no one could see me.

I looked into the pile of stuff that had been stashed beside the house years ago, and there, right in front of me, was the red object I had spotted. It was an old motorcycle that had been covered with a piece of carpet, which had long since rotted away. The rearview mirrors had protruded through, as the carpet had rotted and sagged. The red I could see was the fuel tank. It was a nice colour. There was a large, old, Perspex windshield lying over the seat to protect it, and the entire thing was covered with smelly, rotting leaves.

I reached out and took a corner of the carpet in both hands to lift it up, in order to take a better look at the red tank. It was wet and heavy. I slowly peeled it upwards until my arms were at a full stretch above my head. There was an oval emblem on the tank with the letters BSA inside it. The carpet was really heavy because it was in two layers.

The BSA unveiling

Suddenly the bottom layer totally ripped apart and fell off, leaving me standing, holding the top, drier layer. As the bottom layer came apart, it slapped against my chest, and fell to my feet. I glanced down and realized, to my horror that it was seething with white worms and black beetles. I jumped back with fright; the carpet slapped down on the old motorcycle, squashing and spilling the worms and beetles everywhere. I spun around quickly and ran in a panic for the sunny side of the street. Once there, I managed to flick the worms off my shirt with my finger. The beetles were scurrying about on my pants and shoes. I quickly snapped a leafy twig from a bush and brushed off all the beetles I could find. I stayed on the sunny side of the street all the way to Wingnut's house. I crossed the road again and walked down the narrow path that led to the back of his house.

Wingnut's mom was outside hanging her washing on a clothesline. One end of the line was tied to a tree, and the other end was attached to the corner of the house by a huge screw with a loop on the end. There was a long stick with a V-notch cut into the end of it, to prop the line up higher once everything had been hung in place, to prevent the sheets and things from dragging on the ground. Wingnut was taking the laundry from the basket and handing it to his mom so she could peg it onto the line. She was stretching up to her full reach, with her mouth full of wooden clothes pegs. Wingnut saw me coming through the gate and called out loudly,

"Hey, did you get kicked out of church?"

Wingnut's mom never looked around or reacted to Wingnut's greeting.

I walked up to where Wingnut was untangling a shirt from the laundry basket.

"Hey, Wingnut," I whispered in my quietest voice, "is your mom deaf?"

"Yes," Wingnut declared loudly. "She can't hear anything at all. She got really sick when she was a little girl, and she's been deaf ever since. We talk in sign language, and she knows exactly what I am saying."

"Can she talk?" I whispered.

"Yeah, but she can't hear what her voice sounds like, so the sounds don't come out right, but I know what she says."

I thought for a moment of the first time I had met her, and

remembered how I had felt quite scared of her. Now this explained everything.

I helped Wingnut hand his mom the laundry until it was all hung out on the line. The weight of the wet clothes caused a huge sag in the line, until Wingnut's mom grabbed the prop-up pole and pushed the top end up, and the bottom end under, in one easy motion. This lifted the clothes way off the ground, where they freely billowed up, flapping back and forth in the warm breeze.

Using little signs that he made with his fingers, Wingnut asked his mom if he could go and play now. She nodded in agreement, and Wingnut and I darted off out through his gate and onto the street before she could change her mind.

Without a suggestion, or making any kind of decision, we both walked silently across to the sunny side of the street, and headed towards the bridge that crosses the drain. As we passed the house with all the big trees, I told Wingnut about the BSA, and all the slimy, white worms and the beetles. Wingnut laughed so hard that he winced, as the effort of laughing pulled on the bandage that he had put on his punctured bum.

"Ahh! Don't make me laugh," he stammered. "It hurts." The expression on his face was quite hilarious, as he tightly puckered up his mouth and squinted his eyes, until his eyebrows both sloped up at a steep angle towards the centre of his face. I started laughing uncontrollably and slapped my hands on my knees as I doubled over with hysterical laughter. I was laughing so hard I slapped my knees again; my hand missed, and slapped down on one of the cuts on my leg.

"Ahh! That hurts" I yelled. Wingnut totally cracked up at that, and there we were, both standing in the middle of the sidewalk, doubled over with laughter and wincing with pain at the same time. It's a good thing it was Sunday morning and there was nobody about, because we must have looked a crazy sight.

CHAPTER 9

At the secluded spot at the back of my garage, I told Wingnut about my idea of Operation Payback. He didn't move or say anything. Steadily his face lit up into his full-faced grin.

"That's a great idea. That's the best ever—let's do it."

We pulled my bike out from beside the garage and together we tipped it upside down, put the new wheel on and tightened up the axle nuts. Wingnut spun the wheel with his hand and it ran straight and true. We spent the rest of the morning straightening out all the bent bits and pieces from the Shulak attack, and then I took it for a test ride. It worked as well as ever.

Wingnut watched intently, as I pedaled up and down my driveway, testing the brakes and checking for wobbles and squeaks.

"Hey!" Wingnut shouted at the top of his voice, scaring me half to death. "Let's build an armoured bike, and see if we can teach those nasty Shulaks a lesson."

"Yeah!" I yelled in agreement, as I sped off on my bike as fast as I could go around to the back of the garage, with Wingnut running flat out behind me. I leaned my bike against the little tree, and Wingnut and I rummaged through all the bits and pieces that were lying beside the garage. We pulled out various pieces of this and that, but there was nothing that gave us any inspiration.

"I think we need a plan," I said to Wingnut as he heaved on a small piece of rolled up chicken wire. He stopped pulling and said,

"We should look at the story in the war comic and see if we can get some ideas."

"Yeah that's a great idea. Let's go to your house and get it," I said, as we both ran out through the gap in the poplar hedge and headed off through the long grass in front of old Mac's house.

We ran all the way to Wingnut's house and sped through the gate into the backyard. Wingnut's mom was at the back of the yard and didn't see us dash into the house. We burst into Wingnut's room, where he dove under his bed and retrieved his box of comics, quickly rummaging through them to find the Operation Payback edition. He stuffed it inside his shirt, did up the buttons, and we ran out of the house, through the gate, and all the way down the street to the back of my garage.

We sat down among the bits and pieces that we had strewn about on the small lawn and Wingnut turned to the page where the story started. We sat cross-legged on the grass, shoulder-to-shoulder, and began looking at the pictures and reading the captions one by one. We excitedly skipped through the first part and slowed down to concentrate and think when we came to the part where the soldiers began to build the armoured cab on the truck. Together, we studied the details of the story while our eyes glanced away from the comic, to survey the collection of potential construction material around us.

The story led us to realize that we needed to build a fairly sturdy box around my bike. We placed the comic book at the foot of the little apple tree and rummaged once more through the assortment of stuff beside the garage. The roll of fine chicken wire had some potential, and there were some small pieces of thin plywood that seemed both light and strong, but nothing large enough to cover a boy on a bike. We stopped once more to think, as our enthusiasm for the project was fading rapidly. Wingnut picked up the comic once more and walked over to my bike, with the comic open at the picture of the armoured truck in one hand and his chin cupped in the other, in his most thoughtful pose.

"We need some nice pieces of wood to build a frame first," he said suddenly.

"Well, there's plenty of wood and stuff we could use at the dump if you want to risk puncturing your bum again to go and get it."

"Very funny indeed," Wingnut replied grumpily. "By the way, we'll have to jump the drain again if you want to risk going for another swim." Neither of us laughed, as we both remembered our experiences from the day before. The thoughtful moment evaporated, and we turned at the same time and said,

"Let's go." We started to laugh at our jinx and our motivation was jump started.

Since Wingnut was already wearing his gumboots, I ran to the house and put on mine.

"Let's bring this piece of rope and hammer," said Wingnut, waving a length of rolled up yellow rope and a hammer that he had retrieved from the garage.

We set off once more in the direction of Wingnut's secret shortcut, climbed over the fence with the barbed wire on it, and walked hurriedly down the narrow track between the drain and the small ditch. We stopped and peered down into the scungy water in silence, as the memories of my gashed-up leg and my fall into the water came flashing back.

"My bum hurts," Wingnut said, breaking the thoughtful silence. "I don't think I can make the jump."

"Me neither," I replied with relief, as Wingnut began lowering himself over the concrete edge of the drain, skidding the toes of his boots down the side as he stretched out to his full length, reaching for the bottom. He let go of the edge and dropped the remaining six inches, making a small splash as his boots struck the water. I did the same, and we easily waded across to the other side, with the water only halfway up our boots.

To our dismay, there were no pipes or holes in this area of the drain. We could find no foothold anywhere in sight to enable us to climb out. We were trapped in the drain with no way out. I was thinking that we would have to walk the entire distance back to the bridge, so we could get our toes in the pipes there, to climb out. Wingnut said,

"Give me a leg up, then I'll pull you out."

Wingnut stood on one leg, raising the other, as I cupped my hands together so he could stand in my clasped hands. I could feel all the slime from the bottom of his boots squishing through my fingers, as he put his full weight in my hands. He stood up, grasped the topside of the drain, and easily pulled himself out. He turned and offered me his hand. I grabbed it immediately, but it was still covered with slime and muck from his boots. Instinctively, he rapidly pulled it back and wiped it in the long grass. I wiped mine on my pants and offered it to Wingnut once more, for him to pull me out. He heaved with all his strength as I kicked and scrambled with the toes of my boots, searching for some grip on the concrete side, to help us. Wingnut was straining backwards, pulling on my arm with both feet braced against the lip of the concrete side. I could feel the concrete grating and scratching painfully into my chest, as Wingnut pulled determinedly on my arm. I winced and struggled to get out. Finally, my free hand grabbed the top edge. Wingnut let go of my hand and grabbed hold of my shirt, as I managed to hoist myself up onto my elbows, then swing my leg out to roll safely into the grass.

We found the place in the hedge we had passed through previously, and set off towards the dump. The overturned go-cart was still lying in the grass where we had left it at the bottom of the hill. We wasted no time clambering over the amazing pile of junk, in search of suitable building materials.

This place was a treasure trove of stuff we could use. We quickly gathered a good assortment of manageable lengths of wood. The hammer was the best thing ever, to bash things free and to pull out all the dangerous nails from the pieces that we had selected.

As we surveyed the damage we had made from smashing all the windows, we walked around the area where we had propped up the frames. The shattered glass was scattered everywhere, and it crackled, splintered and popped as we walked on it. We found two small window frames that were covered with metal bug screens. They were in good shape, so we put them on top of the pile of stuff we had collected. Searching far and wide, we found a full sheet of thin plywood. It was unbroken and had three rows of nails sticking through it, which we quickly pulled out with the hammer. It was painted brown on one side and was bare on the other.

We both agreed it was perfect, so taking an end each, we carried it back to our collection pile.

"How are we going to get this across the drain?" I commented, as we surveyed the load we had accumulated.

"Perhaps we could find another way home," Wingnut said, as his eyes scanned off into the distance, in the opposite direction from which we had come.

"Let's walk over there towards those trees for a while, and see if we can find a better way to get all this stuff back to your place." We circled around the edge of the gigantic hole where all the junk was dumped, and waded through the long grass toward a line of very tall poplar trees that we could see in the distance. The grass was riddled with tall thistles, which grabbed and clawed at our clothes as we brushed through them.

Eventually we arrived at the foot of the tall trees and decided to climb up one of them, to get a better view of what lay ahead, so we could get an idea as to what direction we should go. We both managed to climb the tree easily, despite our crusty wounds and my freshly grazed chest. We were in a place neither of us had been before. In the distance we could see several rows of houses in a different neighbourhood than our own.

Suddenly, off to our left, we heard a scream, then another and another. We froze motionless in the leafy tree, hidden from sight among the thick, green mass of leaves. We saw three boys being chased by two older, larger boys. The three younger ones were obviously terrified, as they were screaming in fear as they ran. The older boys were gaining on them rapidly and they soon caught up with their prey.

The small boys were foot-tripped as they ran, or pushed from behind, which sent them sprawling headfirst into the hard-packed ground. There were three paper kites lying on the ground. They were obviously homemade: two were made of newspaper and one was made from brown wrapping paper. The kite tails were made from pairs of old pantyhose and stockings tied together.

As we sat hidden in the tree, we could see that the kites had been smashed and broken as though they had been stomped on, and kicked to pieces. The older boys both wore black ski hats and denim vests. They were slapping and hitting the three boys, who were now screaming and crying. One of the boys bravely picked up a stick and whacked one of the attackers on the head, which sent his hat flying off into the grass. The other attacker left his victims and violently ripped the stick from the boy's hands, whacking the kid with it five times. He then proceeded to tie the kid up with one of the kite tails. The other two tried to escape, but the one who had lost his ski hat ran after them, dragged them back, and tied them up with the other two kite tails.

The three kids were all screaming at the top of their lungs. The attackers ripped off one shoe from each kid, tore off a sock, stuffed it into their mouths and bound it in place by winding the pantyhose around their heads. The three small boys had their hands tied behind their backs and their feet bound together. The attackers left them lying in the grass. The tall one turned to retrieve his hat, and the sunlight lit up his bright red hair.

"It's the Shulaks," Wingnut whispered cautiously, as he clutched my arm in dread. The Shulaks walked off into the distance, leaving the terrified boys tied up, struggling face down in the grass.

Once the Shulaks were safely out of sight, Wingnut and I climbed down from the tree and made our way quietly to where the three boys lay whimpering on the ground. One had a small cut on his head from being hit with the stick, but apart from being terrorized, they were fairly unhurt.

We set about untying the boys. First we untied the stockings around their heads and pulled the socks from their mouths. All the moisture from their mouths had been absorbed by the socks, and they gasped, gagged and sucked on their tongues to find some relief. We untied their hands and helped them to their feet. The youngest one was still sobbing breathlessly. The eldest was about the same age as Wingnut and me, and the blood from the cut on his head was beginning to clot and dry in his hair.

He was constantly looking around, expecting the Shulaks to return. The third boy was filthy dirty from falling head first into the hard, dusty ground when he was foot-tripped by one of the Shulaks. He had grazes on his chin, both knees, and both hands, but he appeared to be quite unaffected by his condition. He dusted himself off with his hands and walked over to where his broken kite lay in pieces on the ground. He held up the remains, and the broken pieces hung limply, in an unrecognizable, dangling mess.

"I knew I should have made the kite tail longer," he said.

Wingnut and I both turned toward him in surprise, as the other two boys began to chuckle in amusement. He went on to explain that when they were making their kites that morning, his big sister told him that the tail of the newly-constructed kite was too short, and that it would loop around and around without the stability of a longer tail. Of course, he couldn't make it too obvious that he would take the advice of a girl, so he declared that it was perfect the way it was, as he and his two friends rushed out the door with their new kites in hand.

They had them flying fairly high, when they first spotted the two Shulak brothers, walking aimlessly across the huge field. Suddenly, the short-tailed kite caught some extra wind and began to loop around and around in circles uncontrollably, until it crashed into the ground just an arm's length in front of the Shulaks. They instantly flew into a rage, trampled the kite to pieces, and ran wildly towards the other two boys, who still had kites in the air, snatching the string from their hands. One of the brothers held the end of the kite string, while the other ran towards the kite with the taut string under his arm, dragging it from the sky. As soon as it was within his reach, he smashed it to bits. They quickly repeated the same activity with the third kite.

Apparently the older boy had managed to plant a really good kick on the backside of one of the Shulaks as he was bending over to rip one of the kites apart. This sent them into another flaming rage, and that's what started all the screaming that Wingnut and I had heard from the tree.

Once the three boys had recovered from their ordeal, they introduced themselves as Ken, Rob and Paul. All five of us sat in a circle in the grass, as Wingnut and I told them of our encounters with the Shulaks, and our preparations for Operation Payback. Ken, the eldest, told us that they had seen the Shulak brothers bullying and robbing kids in their neighbourhood from time to time, and he was sure he could round up plenty of kids from his school to help with Operation Payback.

Ken, Rob and Paul stashed their kite string under a tree and said they would come back to get it later, after they helped Wingnut and me get our collection of building materials back to my house, in thanks for rescuing them.

We tied all the pieces of wood together with the yellow rope, and placed the bundle on top of the sheet of plywood.

Using some old nails, we hammered a short frame together and nailed the plywood on top of it. Wingnut ran over to the spot where the overturned go-cart lay in the grass at the bottom of the hill. He quickly flipped it over and gasped in astonishment, as he saw that the nail that had punctured his bum had a small fragment of his blood-soaked pants stuck to it, and a small flap of his skin.

He trundled the cart over to the collection of stuff, and we placed the whole lot, plywood and all, onto the cart and towed it easily through the grass.

The boys knew of a disused service road that wound its way along the back of the houses. It was somewhat overgrown with weeds and clumps of grass, but it had been packed hard by much use many years ago.

CHAPTER 10

The old road led erratically around piles of dirt which were overgrown with weeds, small trees and bushes. The surface gravel was becoming progressively looser, and was now creating a small cloud of dust behind us as we walked along. The youngest boy, Paul, said that he was getting very thirsty, as his mouth was still terribly dry from having his sock stuffed into it. We all laughed at his complaint but in fact, it had become very hot as the sun had risen high in the cloudless sky above us. We were all in need of a cool drink.

As we rounded a curve in the road, we all stopped dead in our tracks with dismay. Before us was a huge, metal, chain link gate, with barbed wire strung along the top of it. A large, rusty chain hung from a massive padlock in the centre; our way was barred.

Through the gate, we could see that we were only a short distance from my street, as I recognized two of the houses which I could see from where I stood.

We all stood motionless in the sun, on the old dusty road, and pondered the predicament of how to get through, around, under, or over the huge gate in front of us. One by one we approached the gate and considered a strategy of how to conquer it.

Wingnut's idea of bashing the padlock with the hammer until it broke was probably the best idea, but we didn't want to attract any unwanted attention by the noise it would create.

I gazed away, to the left of the gate, and noticed that the fence, which extended from both sides of the gate, only went a short distance in that direction. Behind it was a long row of huge trees, which formed the property boundaries at the back of the houses that faced the street. A shallow drainage ditch ran all the way along the boundary at the foot of the trees. The land beside us was clear of all weeds, bushes, and long grass; it was an open, green pasture, dotted with the occasional cow munching nonchalantly on the short, lush grass at its feet.

"We can go that way," I said, breaking the silence and interrupting the thoughts of the small group beside me. We turned the loaded go-cart to our left and headed for the open pasture. It was easy going, except for the scattered cow poops that were difficult to avoid. They were as large as dinner plates with a dry crust on the top, like a freshly baked pie.

The centre was a thick, gooey, dark paste that clung to everything it touched. It didn't take long until the spokes of the wheels on our cart were completely clogged with dripping, oozing cow dung. Our gumboots looked just the same except the inside edges of the tops of our boots were smeared, slippery, smooth, and shiny, from rubbing together as we walked. Ken, Rob and Paul, however, were all wearing regular school shoes which offered no resistance to the cow poop as it oozed over the tops and slopped its way down inside, making their socks thick and clingy each time they inadvertently stepped in some.

As we progressed through the cow pasture, traversing along parallel with the row of trees and the shallow drainage ditch, the grass at our feet gradually became longer and longer, and there was a noticeable absence of cow turds. It was as if the cows had completely avoided this area of the expansive field.

"Listen!" Rob declared, as he put his right arm in the air to silence us all. We stopped in our tracks in response to the signal, with startled expressions and ears straining, to catch the slightest sound. Motionless for several seconds, we detected a dull, throbbing, chant-like sound, which had a regular but distinct pulse to it.

Rob lowered his hand slowly as we continued walking in silence. The regular, pulsing, throbbing sound, continued to get louder.

"I see it!" Ken yelled, startling everyone into a frozen stance. "It's an electric fence—no wonder none of the cows come here to graze; they all keep well away from it." The fence was nothing more than two strands of wire, stretched tight across the field. It was held up with widely-spaced metal fence posts, with white ceramic loops crimped into them, through which the wires passed.

"How can a fence be electric?" Rob asked. Ken, being the eldest of the group, guessed that the wires must be plugged into something, somewhere. He informed our group of attentive listeners that the cows get a shock from it if they touch it, so they stay away from it after they have been zapped a time or two.

"How much of a shock would they get?" Rob asked.

"I don't know," Ken replied, "just a tingle I would expect. Let's test it." He stooped to pick a long, broad, blade of grass from between his feet. He held the grass between his thumb and forefinger at one end, and touched the wire with the other. In half a second, the wire pulsed, and sent an electric current up the grass, making his hand clench shut. Luckily the grass slipped off the wire, preventing him from getting the next jolt of electricity. He yelped with surprise at the intensity, and clutched his throbbing hand between his legs.

We watched with fascination and excitement, and Ken bravely pretended that it wasn't really too bad.

"Why don't you guys try it," he challenged. There was no comment or reply, until Wingnut broke the silence.

"Let's pee on it," he said, "I'll bet it will make sparks and stuff and look really cool."

Little Paul was the first one to unzip his pants, take out his diddle, and make himself ready to pee on the wire. He screwed up his face in concentration as he strained to conjure up some pee. Suddenly, he gave a little shiver as the warm stream began to flow. His aim took a little adjusting as he raised the angle a bit by bending his knees and tilting his hips to get a little more height.

"You missed!" Wingnut shouted, as Paul made another adjustment to the angle, which put him with his hips thrust forward and his back arched back so far that he had to go on his tiptoes to keep his balance.

Suddenly he exploded backwards, as if he had been shot with a high powered rifle. His feet came clear off the ground, as his hips flew back, folding him in half like a book being slammed shut. He hit the ground face first and lay there clutching himself.

The electric current had travelled up his stream of pee and had given him a jolt big enough to make a cow jump in the air. Cows get enough of a shock through their thick skin and coarse hair to make them never forget. But poor wee Paul got zapped right on his most delicate part. All the muscles in the lower half of his body were clenching and unclenching involuntarily.

"I guess you would have to pee on both wires at once to make a spark," Wingnut blurted out jokingly, breaking the concerned silence. We all laughed heartily, except little Paul, who was on the verge of tears from pain and shock. It took him nearly twenty minutes to recover enough to stand up. He was walking a little funny, so we all agreed that he should ride on top of the pile of stuff that was tied to the go-cart.

We slipped easily under the bottom strand of pulsing, electrified wire. Little Paul just laid out flat and stiff in the grass, as we slid him under the fence like a pizza going into an oven.

Eventually we came upon a small gap in the row of trees that someone had made, to use as a shortcut to their house.

"It's old man Scott's house," I announced, as soon as I had spotted the old hothouse made of glass, which had all sorts of plants and vines growing all around it. It was made of square panes of glass, held together with a white wooden framework. It had been there for years, and the plants that surrounded it were all mature and healthy. The property backed onto the small drainage ditch that we had been following, and the row of trees formed a huge, dense border at the property boundary.

The front of the house was exactly opposite my house, which was on the other side of the street.

"Could we cross through their back yard to get to your house?" Wingnut asked.

"Yes, there's a small garden path that goes all the way past that glasshouse, down beside their house, to the street. But we had better not take any shortcuts through old man Scott's garden. He's a nasty old coot who wouldn't hesitate to give us all a thrashing with a stick, if he caught us trespassing."

"Maybe there's no one home," Ken exclaimed. "Let's go take a look." Within seconds, Ken and Wingnut had slipped through the gap in the trees and had disappeared into old man Scott's backyard. The rest of our group sat in the grass waiting nervously for their return.

Inside the garden, Ken and Wingnut found themselves in a wonderland of flowers and vegetables. The dense growth around them shielded them from view, from any angle. There were tall rows of waving corn, green peas growing on crisscrossed sticks, tomatoes, carrots, cabbages and all manner of tall and short plants. There were fruit trees growing so close together that they formed an unbroken shady canopy. The little garden path led past the door of the glasshouse, then took a sharp left turn to traverse across the property, to an old wooden garage that was also overgrown with thick, leafy vines.

The two boys were sneaking silently on their tiptoes in a low crouch, like a couple of stalking cats. As they rounded the corner, which was bordered by thick, overgrown black current bushes, Ken stopped and looked back over his shoulder to check if Wingnut was still close behind. Wingnut was so intent on trying to sneak silently that he crashed into Ken, who was so startled, he let out a frightened yelp, which scared Wingnut so much he just waved his arms about and began sprinting on the spot. Ken clutched his hand over his racing heart and stood still to catch his breath. Wingnut began puffing and blowing and pacing about on the spot. Neither spoke until the colour had returned to their faces and their pulses had returned to normal. They turned back in the direction of the glasshouse for better cover, and prepared to make a run for it if anyone had detected their presence.

A calm silence fell over the little garden, as the boys recovered. The wind dropped, and the sun slipped behind a cloud, throwing everything under a subdued shadow. The garden was transformed in an instant, to a gloomy, forbidding place where they knew they should not be.

Cautiously and silently, the two boys edged their way toward the house. They crouched behind the cover of the black current bushes and sat motionless, as they spied on old man Scott's house for signs of life. Several drawn-out minutes passed with no sign of movement near the house. They could see into the kitchen through the window, and saw no signs of movement in there, either. Ken signaled Wingnut to follow him, and they bravely crept closer and closer to the house. As they came up beside the garage, Ken stood on an old upturned plastic bucket, and cupped his hands around his eyes to peer through the garage window.

"The car's gone," Ken whispered in excitement, "let's get the others and get out of here while the going's good." They raced down the garden path, and ducked out through the gap in the trees, into the sunlight on the other side.

We soon had the load on the go-cart rearranged so it would fit through the gap in the trees. The five of us easily carried it across the little ditch, stuffed it through the trees, and placed it down quietly on the garden path. With two boys in front and three behind, it rode smoothly on the little path. We brushed past all the overhanging plants and moved a garden hose out of our way. Rob stopped as he drew alongside the glasshouse. He was staring through the glass, examining the interior.

"Take a look at this," he beckoned quietly, and we all peered through the glass.

"What are those things?" Rob asked, as we all strained in an effort to make out what was growing on the vines inside.

"They're giant grapes!" Ken declared. "They're huge! Let's pick a few," he challenged, as he strode towards the door of the glasshouse.

Clutching the handle, he realized that the door was locked. He quickly walked around to the end of the greenhouse and spotted a small ventilation window that was open. It was hinged at the top, and was held in its open position by a metal arm with a series of holes in it, which fitted over a small pin so that it could be adjusted. It was set high in the wall, but Ken could see a huge bunch of the massive grapes hanging just within arm's reach of the window. He darted off and returned with the plastic bucket that he had stood on to see into the garage. He dumped it upside down and climbed onto it, grappling his arm through the little window as far as he could reach. He was not quite high enough to extend his arm all the way. Jumping down, he grabbed little Paul, hoisted him up into his arms, and then stood up on the bucket. Paul struggled and kicked to get down as he was still throbbing from having his penis electrocuted earlier.

Ken lowered him to the ground and impatiently gestured to Rob to get up on his shoulders. Caught up in the excitement of the moment, obediently Rob nimbly climbed onto Ken's shoulders, as he squatted down to let him do so. Once settled into the precariously high position, he held Ken's head with both hands, as his mount climbed carefully once more onto the upturned bucket. As he was manoeuvred into position, it was an easy matter to reach his arm through the open window and clasp his hand around the largest bunch of grapes within reach.

Two dull thuds reverberated from the front of the garden: the unmistakable sound of car doors closing.

"Old man Scott's home!" Wingnut warned in his loudest quiet voice. We all darted about on the spot, looking for an escape route and following each other's lead like a flock of startled birds.

Rob quickly withdrew his arm from the window, clutching a huge bunch of grapes, as Ken hurriedly stepped down from the bucket in response to Wingnut's warning. In the same instant, Rob's rolled-up sleeve caught fast on the little pin that protruded from the sill to permit the positioning of the window.

Ken had already dismounted from the bucket, and Rob was torn from Ken's shoulders in a flurry of kicking legs.

A man's deep voice reverberated around the garden, as Mr. Scott declared that he would go to the garden and pick some peas and tomatoes for dinner. The words were no sooner spoken than a huge, elongated man's shadow slithered silently along the garden path and wiggled its way up and over the tops of the vegetables, as Mr. Scott emerged into the garden behind it.

Trapped at the glasshouse

Terrified we were not shielded from view by the glass house, Paul had squeezed himself into a narrow space between the glasshouse and the tall wooden fence that bordered the property. The rest of us followed him into the hiding space, except for Rob, who was still hanging by his right arm, like a dressed-up wind chime.

Ken whispered a blunt instruction for him to keep perfectly still. Mr. Scott meandered lazily down the garden path, and commenced to efficiently pick the abundant, green peas that were growing in a tangled leafy row before him.

He casually placed the peas in a small white pail that he held in his other hand, and sauntered off the path, disappearing between the rows of high tomato plants. We huddled in hot, clammy silence, in our airless gap. Rob hung limp and lifeless. The blood had left his arm from the elbow down, and he had dropped the stolen grapes as soon as his hand had gone to sleep.

Old man Scott took his sweet time picking his vegetables. He putzed about, plucking the odd weed here and there, as they caught his casual attention.

He did not venture far enough into the garden to see Rob hanging like and abandoned scarecrow from his glasshouse window.

Eventually, he plodded off towards the house, with his little pail of harvest goodies, and disappeared inside, with a positive click of the door behind him.

We exhaled with relief, and began to un-jam ourselves from our constricted hiding place, emerging slowly, one by one. Ken grabbed Rob by his hips, and lifted most of his weight, which allowed Rob to unhook his shirtsleeve. They both came down onto the ground together, with a sigh of relief.

Rob's hand was blue and lifeless, and his fingers didn't respond to any direction given to them by his brain.

The lengthening shadows all around us indicated that it was now late afternoon. We huddled together at the back of the glasshouse to decide what to do about our predicament. Little Paul noticed that Mrs. Scott had drawn the curtains on the side of the house facing the garage, and had closed the

Venetian blinds facing the back. Luckily, once again, we were out of sight. We hurriedly organized the go-cart to ensure the load was not going to rattle or fall off. We placed Paul on top of the heap as before, where he sat cross-legged, clutching his throbbing privates with his left hand, and holding onto the tie-down rope with the other.

With two in front, two behind, and one on top, we silently moved the go-cart with nervous stealth, closer and closer to the house. As we rounded the corner by the black current bushes, we could see in front of us a straight run between the garage and the house, all the way to the open street beyond. With racing pulses and quickened breath, we hurriedly picked up speed and passed the house unseen. We emerged out onto the street with the elated grins of relieved escapees.

We thanked our three new pals for helping us. Standing in the semi-darkness, we waved as Ken, Rob and Paul walked off solemnly down the street in single file, in the direction of their suburb, with little Paul lagging wearily behind, still suffering from his traumatic afternoon.

Wingnut and I quietly turned the go-cart, with its load still intact, up our driveway and parked it in seclusion behind the garage. Wingnut bid me goodbye and with a backward wave of his hand called out,

"See you tomorrow."

CHAPTER 11

It was the first day of summer holidays. All the kids were so excited to finally be off school. They tidied their desks, cleaned out their lockers, and ran for the door as soon as the final school bell rang. Dozens of groups of kids streamed noisily out of the school gates, riding their bikes like schools of fish all grouped together. Some walked, some waited for their bus, and some climbed into their parents' cars, which were all loaded up for camping holidays, visiting grandparents, or other trips to who knows where. I climbed onto my bike and marveled at how well it worked since Wingnut and I fixed it up and put on the new wheel. I followed a small group of kids on bikes at a distance. The girls were all riding together, talking and laughing with each other as they went. The boys were pedaling along behind, fooling about playfully between themselves, as the two happy groups made their way home.

Alone with my thoughts, I biked along, thinking of the first day I had taken Wingnut's secret shortcut home, and all the adventures that had happened since. It seemed as if it had all happened a long time ago.

I hadn't noticed that I had drifted far behind the group of kids I was following. I had been putting less and less effort into pedaling, as I became more and more engrossed in my thoughts. As I looked up, I was surprised to see that the kids had all veered off the road and were hurriedly crossing over onto the grassy centre of the avenue heading for the trees. They seemed to be bent over their handlebars and pedaling very hard. I suddenly realized that these kids were all fleeing from an attack by the Shulaks.

This was the exact place Wingnut and I had been bombarded with clumps of earth just a few days earlier. It was like watching an action replay. The Shulaks were carrying small buckets in their left hands, while their right hands dipped rapidly into the pails to grab handfuls of ripe crabapples. They flung them repeatedly at the two small groups of kids. The older brother was pelting the boys, and the younger one ran after the girls, hurling handfuls of half-rotten apples at them as fast as he could grab them from the pail. The girls screamed in horror as the crabapples splattered all about them, exploding in a brown, stinking mess as they struck their backs, legs and heads.

Many of the girls had large gobs of slimy, rotten apple muck plastered in their hair, which plopped onto their blouses as they frantically pedaled to get away.

The two Shulaks pursued the cyclists until they had thrown all of their ammunition. I stopped my bike behind a thick leafy bush at the end of someone's driveway to watch the attack. The Shulaks turned to cross the avenue, walking and laughing all the way back to their house, just as they had done with Wingnut and me.

"That's it!" I gasped to myself. "That's their trap; that's where we can head them off at the pass, when we launch Operation Payback."

Once the Shulaks had disappeared behind the stone wall at the front of their house, I sped off after the two groups of kids, who had stopped just around the corner to clean themselves off.

The girls were all crying as they attempted to pick the larger gobs of rotten muck from their hair, and flick the other sticky bits off their backs and legs.

The boys also were busying themselves in an attempt to clean up. One or two of them looked as if they were about to cry and probably would have, if they had been alone.

A tall skinny girl dropped her bike on the ground and came striding towards the boys. Her face was flushed with anger, and her expression was that of a snarling wolf. She was quite hysterical as she hurled a barrage of abuse at the boys, demanding to know why they hadn't done something to defend the girls during the attack. One brave soul stepped forward, and boldly stated that they were under attack also, and not only that, there were two of them. The tall girl went berserk, waving her arms about in a frustrated gesture as she screamed at the lad who had spoken.

"There were eight of you, and only two of them!" The boy blinked at the volume and the tone, and began to stammer a forced reply.

"Well, they're tough guys and they're really bad guys as well. They would probably have beaten us all up if we had tried to do anything."

"He's right," I blurted out confidently as I strode through the small crowd of kids and stood facing the girls' self-appointed spokesperson. She glared down at me, still wearing the snarly frown.

"What do you know?" she snapped.

"Well, I know the same thing happened to my friend and me, except we were hit with rock-hard clumps of dirt, my bike was stomped to death, and my friend's money was stolen."

Like a sign from the gods, Wingnut's solitary sock was dangling from the tree right above us.

"See," I pointed with a dramatic, evangelical flourish, "there's my friend's sock that they ripped from his foot."

There were eighteen kids, all standing in silence, staring like the faithful at the omen, which was Wingnut's crusty sock.

The tall girl had begun to soften a little and her face, colour and expressions returned to normal.

"We should call the police," she announced.

"And tell them what?" the brave boy asked. "That some bullies threw rotten apples at us?" She looked a little flustered and retorted,

"Well something should be done to fix those *%*!" I'm not sure exactly what the word she used meant, but it sounded really appropriate and very descriptive.

A shocked silence fell over the crowd, so I spoke.

"We already have a plan," I stated boldly.

"We? Who's 'we'?" the tall girl blurted.

"My friend and I," I replied. "The plan's called Operation Payback. Perhaps you would all like to help us with the plan."

It was a wonderful moment. I found myself at the centre of attention, sharing our secret plan with the entire captivated crowd. The stench of rotten apples was a little overwhelming, as the kids crowded closer to me while I described the details.

The mood of the crowd had now changed from shock and anger to enthusiastic excitement.

"When shall we do it?" the skinny spokesperson demanded.

"I don't know. Now that school is out, we won't be coming here for a while."

"Yes we will," she chirped, "the Saturday after next is our school fair, and we'll all be riding our bikes to that, won't we?" she demanded of the crowd. They all agreed.

"Let's all meet in the middle of that park over there, this Saturday, to finalize the plan."

"That's tomorrow," the brave boy challenged.

"Well, Wednesday then, at one o'clock," the tall girl stated defensively.

A murmur of agreement rippled over the small crowd as they mounted their bikes and cycled home. I felt like a commander of the troops as I rode home alone, with my head filled with strategies and manoeuvres and an overwhelming sense of the excited anticipation of battle.

The air was warm and carried the scent of many different flowers, as Wingnut and I sat in our headquarters under the apple tree at the back of our garage, among the excellent collection of stuff we had accumulated. We felt safe and private here; for some reason, this was not a part of our back yard that was visited by my mom and dad. We tried to keep our supplies tidy and hidden from the enemy, but some of the pieces were pretty big and difficult to disguise. Our operations room was under the sheet of plywood that we had propped up against the garage. It was held in place with two sturdy boards at each end that were nailed to it to form an "A" frame. This was now the war room.

We had a sturdy box with a flat piece of wood placed on top of it, located in the centre of our makeshift room, and this was now our battle-planning table.

With a large pad, a pencil, and a plastic ruler, we drew a plan of the avenue where the Shulaks had attacked us and the other kids. The map included the Shulaks' house, the park, and both side streets that led onto the avenue. It was a masterpiece in the making, as Wingnut and I added all the details of the area as we thought of them.

We could not agree on the location of the small gate that led into the tennis courts, where Wingnut and I had stopped to catch our breath the day we were attacked.

"Let's go down there and take our map with us to make sure we haven't missed anything."

"Great idea," Wingnut replied as he rolled up our map, gathered up the pencil and ruler, and stuffed all of it in the front of his shirt.

I grabbed my bike, and with Wingnut sitting on the crossbar, we headed down the street to the avenue. We turned left at the little church by Wingnut's house and pedaled with determination down the side road that ran parallel to the avenue. We reached the tennis courts and I parked my bike against the high green fence. There was a high wire mesh wall on top of the fence, all around the tennis courts, to prevent stray balls from flying onto the road. Wingnut pulled out our map, and we soon realized that we were wrong about the location of the gate; we had also missed the side street that ran through the park.

We made the necessary corrections and labeled the side roads Side Street #1 and Side Street #2. We drew in the avenue, the Shulaks' house, and the tennis court gate. The Shulaks' house was in the top left corner, with the stone wall in front it and the sidewalk with the main avenue running past the house.

Three houses to the right was Side Street #1, on the same side of the avenue as the Shulaks' house. At the far side of the avenue, the large grass-covered verge was drawn in, including the trees. At the bottom of the map was the park with Side Street #2 and the park gate near the centre. The tennis courts were located in the far right bottom corner.

We stood in the morning sun, with our backs to the tennis court gate. Through the evenly spaced trees, we could see the Shulaks' house with the overgrown, dark foliage, the uncared-for trees and bushes, hanging over the grey stone wall, casting dark, murky shadows. It had the feeling of a haunted castle.

With the revised map safely stowed, and Wingnut on the crossbar, the ride home was silent except for the slight hum of the tyres on the road, and the whirring of the chain going around and around. As we stowed our map, drawing pad and Wingnut's comic into the upturned box in the centre of our new shelter, we heard my dad's car pull quietly up the driveway and come to a stop at the garage door. We sat in silence and listened as the garage doors were unlatched from the inside, and slowly opened to let the car in. The doors were closed and latched, and my dad left through the side door and walked up the path towards the house.

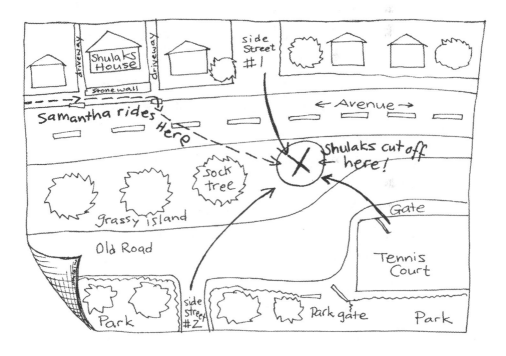

Action plan map

Wingnut and I quickly tidied up all our stuff, before he left through the gap in the poplar trees and disappeared down the little track we'd created through the long grass

After dinner, Mom took me to the hospital again. My brother had gone to scouts on his bike, and my sister had been picked up by her friend's mom to go for a sleepover. I took the drawing pad and pencil with me, and as soon as my mom sat and nattered, I found a quiet corner where I began sketching some different views of an armoured bike. As I drew, I began to realize with excitement that Operation Payback was stirring into a reality. I sketched several different versions of a bike with sides, but it was difficult to visualize the front and the back. I had my head down with my pencil zigzagging back and forth. The rest of my surroundings were shut out, as I concentrated on my drawing. I couldn't wait to show Wingnut the plans. All we had to do was to figure out what we could use from our collection of stuff, and how we could attach it to my bike.

A nurse broke my concentration, startling me as she patted me on the head like a dog. She praised me for being such a good little boy, behaving and entertaining myself while my mother visited. Nobody asked what I was so busy entertaining myself with, nor did they ask to see my sketch. I was greatly relieved when she turned on her heels and walked off, in a business-like manner, with her ample bum cheeks jiggling alternately as she walked.

CHAPTER 12

Woken by the morning sunlight filtering through the curtains, the promise of an interesting day began to emerge in my mind. I could hear that Mom was already up and clattering about in the kitchen. I lay in bed listening to the sounds in the house: dull footsteps, things being clanked together, doors and drawers opening and closing, the muffled sound of the radio babbling the news of the day. A faint odor drifted stealthily into my room; I sniffed the air to detect what it was. A moment later it became a little stronger and my mouth began to fill with saliva, as my senses detected the magnificent smell of bacon cooking. That was the trigger that launched me out of bed.

Mom and Dad paid me pocket money each week for doing work around the house. I was delegated enough jobs to use up my entire Saturday morning. Those jobs were non-negotiable, mandatory tasks that were reviewed in detail for completeness before I could leave the premises. If anything was found to be unsatisfactory, incomplete, or it was discovered that some shortcut or another was taken, it was not uncommon to have your ear grabbed and turned inside out, and be lifted by it until you were on your tiptoes, then led all the way back to the location of the discovered infringement. At this point, the slave master would hover in the background, arms folded, face scowling and ready to pounce, should any further infractions occur or, heaven forbid, if anyone should attempt to make a run for it.

I tried it once. My mom's a little fat, but boy is she quick. I remember her astonishing speed and stamina. She had easily gained on me by the time I reached the end of the driveway. She reached out and grabbed my flapping shirt. Her distinct weight advantage was evident when all the slack was taken up. I was jerked off my feet, and instantly jerked up onto my feet again, and that's when the inside-out ear hold trick was invented.

So as not to invite any undue attention or additional jobs, I hustled through my chores, checking each one over as I completed it. Once finished, I excused myself cautiously and slipped out of sight very quietly, to avoid any further attention.

I rounded the back of the garage and climbed into the confines of our war room to work on the sketch of the armoured bike. Just as I was getting settled and gathering my thoughts to apply them to my bike design, I was stopped in my tracks with a sense of dread, as I heard my mom calling my name from the back door of the house.

It didn't matter how far away I was, or where I was, I could always hear my mom's voice when she called me. She would have been great to have on top of an ambulance yelling "dinner, dinner, dinner!"

I hurried to face the music for whatever it was that I had done or not done. It was always totally unpredictable, as my mom used her special "mom senses" to sniff out problems, and the eyes in the back of the head thing really seemed to help her nail me for something. To my surprise and relief, she told me that Mrs. Scott had asked her over for afternoon tea, and would I like to come with her. I held my breath for a few seconds; I could feel my eyes involuntarily flicking back and forth searching for an answer. My mind was racing to decide if this was perhaps a trick question, that no matter what answer I gave, I would have to go with her. I could hear the clock on the kitchen wall ticking the seconds away as she waited for my reply.

"I was just going to clean my bike and tidy the garage," I blurted out in desperation.

"Oh, well, that's fine dear. I will only be two doors away if you need me. There's a sandwich in the fridge for your lunch." Once again my mom had totally surprised me; once again, I was free to spend the afternoon doing my stuff.

My dad had already gone out to play bowls. I was never quite sure what that actually meant but it was some sort of a game where old folks rolled these shiny balls from one end of a really smooth lawn to the other, and then back again. It didn't seem to be much fun, but it sure seemed to make them fairly thirsty, as they were all always sipping away on cold drinks.

I watched Mom turn left at the end of the driveway. I spun around and darted off at full speed through the hedge, across the field and was running up the slope of the bridge over the drain when I spotted Wingnut walking up the other side, heading to see me. We noticed each other at exactly the same time, and once again we both called out at exactly the same time,

"I've got an idea," followed by a harmonized "jinx." We laughed our heads off again as we both headed off to our operations room, to work on the plans and the sketch for Operation Payback.

Once again we pulled all our hard-earned building materials out from beside the garage, and spread them out on the grass so we could see what we had.

I ran around to the garage side door to get some tools to work with, and as I opened the door I realized that the garage was empty. Wingnut and I carried most of our bits and pieces into the garage and set my bike up in the centre. We started cutting short pieces of wood to make cross braces, and long bits that reached the full length of the bike. We nailed together a complete box frame that fitted all around the outside of the bike. We attached the cross braces at right angles to the cross bar, just behind the handlebars, and one at the back, just behind the seat. Once the frame was built and attached, I climbed onto the bike to see how it fit.

The handlebars were free to move, and the pedals were free to go around. It was just great. We were excited child geniuses, as we hacked away at the sheet of thin plywood, taking turns on the saw when one of us got tired. We cut it exactly in half down the centre and nailed a half sheet on each side of the frame. I sat on the seat again and found that the plywood did not cover my head and shoulders, so we bashed it free and moved it up on the frame, only to realize that now my legs and feet were exposed.

"Let's do the top half first," Wingnut instructed. I ran to the house, grabbed a big glass of milk and my sandwich and we hashed out all the possibilities as we shared my lunch.

We had a sturdy frame and two sides built. We cut a narrow slit at eye level on either side, to provide some visibility. We had found a small bundle of flat wooden slats, which were easy to nail across the back. We didn't even have to cut them to length, as they were already just the right size, by chance. We pushed each slat up tight against the other and nailed it in place.

We were able to stretch the fine chicken wire we had found around the bottom half of the frame. This would provide fairly good protection for the legs and feet, but only for objects larger than the size of the wire netting.

The box was complete except for the front. Visibility was fairly restricted by the plywood sides, so we needed to cover the front part of the box, but we were now out of useable stuff.

We sat side by side on a box with our elbows on our knees and our chins in our hands. We had run out of steam and our momentum had come to a standstill. A sullen silence fell over us both, as we stared at our creation.

"We need a window," Wingnut said, calmly breaking the silence.

"Hey!" he blurted, startling me out of my wits. "Remember the day you got covered in worms and beetles when you found the old BSA under some rotten carpet? That windshield is just what we need."

The sun shone, the breeze was warm, and our enthusiasm was restored as we raced each other through the hedge and sprinted through the long grass towards the drain, where we climbed over the fence and headed down the sunny side of the road. We finally reached the house where the BSA was stashed. We stood on the opposite side of the road to survey the situation.

The spooky old house was barely visible through the overgrown trees and bushes. The whole property looked as dark and gloomy as if it was a secret world, untouched by caring people or sunlight. Wingnut and I squatted in the warm sun, with our backs up against a low stone wall that had also been warmed by the sun. It was a momentarily pleasant place, leaning there with both sides of our bodies feeling warm and comfortable.

Suddenly, a movement on the other side of the road caught our attention; something was moving slowly in the shady darkness beyond. We both raised our hands in a salute to shield our squinting eyes from the sun. Straining with concentration, we detected yet another movement behind the dingy growth across the street. We squatted there motionless as the movement came closer and closer. The leafy vines at the right side of the property moved and parted. There was a faint click, then a loud creak, and the old, half-rotten, wooden gate, with its paint peeling off in flakes, creaked open slowly, scraping a green moss covered arc as it went.

The witch sighting

An ancient bicycle slowly emerged through the gate, pushed by an equally ancient old lady. She was dressed from head to toe in black.

She wore a wide-brimmed hat, which was tied under her withered chin with a black bow. Her long, black dress was covered to her waist by a thin black jacket that was buttoned up to her neck. She emerged slowly and turned to close the gate behind her, even though the gate stood alone among the foliage, without a fence at either side. She mounted her bike as if in slow motion and pedaled laboriously down the shady side of the street, before disappearing out of sight around the corner. We turned to look at each other in disbelief.

"It's a witch," I said into Wingnut's expressionless face.

"Yeah, sure looks like it," Wingnut replied. "Well, she's gone now, let's sneak through the trees and take a look at that old BSA."

"I don't know," I replied, "the last time I went in there it really creeped me out, especially getting covered with worms and beetles."

"It's our only chance," said Wingnut, as he rose to his feet and headed off across the street. I caught up to him as we both slipped through the small gap in the trees into the damp, musty darkness of the overgrown yard.

We darted silently from tree to tree in an attempt to feel hidden from view, pressing our bodies up against each tree as we cautiously peered around its trunk to see if the way was clear. We dashed to the next, then the next, until we reached the old wooden ladder leaning up against the wall.

The piece of rotten carpet lay on the ground where I had dropped it. The seething mass of insects that were all over it the last time I had seen it had migrated away from the daylight, to find a new dark, damp place to live.

We stood and surveyed the scene; it was exactly as I had left it. We each took hold of one end of the rotten carpet and gingerly slid it off the old motorcycle. To our surprise and relief, it was actually quite dry and free from crawling insects. Only the dry and rotting leaves fell to the ground, as we gently placed it down. The old motorcycle had two flat tyres, and it was dusty and dirty, but the carpet cover seemed to have protected it as it wasn't rusty, except for the bits that stuck out through the carpet.

The windshield, which was the treasure we were after, lay on the seat with the curved side up. Wingnut tried to lift it. It seemed to be stuck. He pulled harder, it moved a little, and then he yanked on it with all his might. The motorcycle came free from the wall on which it was leaning and toppled over rapidly. Wingnut was thrown violently backwards, bashing the back of his head hard into my nose as I stood behind him. I fell over backwards with the impact, clutching my stinging nose.

Through a dizzy haze and watering eyes, I could see that the bike had fallen over and had pinned Wingnut underneath it. The windshield had come free in his hands, and had flown over his head and landed on the mossy ground behind him as he fell. Wingnut thrashed about violently, as he tried to lift the bike off his trapped leg by himself, but it was way too heavy. I rushed to help him, but I couldn't do more than make it rock in place, which caused him to call out in pain.

"My leg nearly came free when you did that," he muttered through his clenched teeth, "try it again."

"Hold on a minute," I blurted desperately, as I dashed over and grabbed the old wooden ladder from against the wall and hurriedly dragged it over to where Wingnut lay. I stuffed one end of it under the bike as far as I could, and heaved up with all my strength on the other end. The bike began to tip, so I pushed a little more. Wingnut jerked his body frantically, pulling on his leg.

"A little more," he demanded. I walked my hands down three rungs, which pushed my end even higher. Wingnut jerked violently again and his leg came free.

A blanket of relief covered us both, as we gathered our senses. Wingnut had a hole halfway up his gumboot, where the bike had pinned him. He had a huge red spot on his leg that was beginning to turn into a blue, swollen bruise. He stood up and tried out his leg. It was really sore, but OK to stand on.

The two of us grabbed a place on the motorcycle, one of us at each end, and together with a huge effort we managed to stand it up and shove it back up against the wall where we had found it. I replaced the ladder, and we even spread the old carpet back over the bike.

"Let's get out of here," stated Wingnut urgently, as he stooped to pick up the motorcycle windshield from its resting place. He used his hand to brush off the dead leaves that had long since dried and stuck where they lay. Tucking the windshield under his arm the best he could, we headed to the small gap in the trees through which we had come. As we reached the gap, we paused for a second as Wingnut manipulated the large windshield so he could guide it through the gap. He disappeared through the trees and I followed immediately behind him.

At the very moment we passed through, out into the sunlight we were instantly grabbed on our upper arms with a tight, bony grip, and shaken hard until we faced each other. We were caught in a grasp, and pushed into a position that we couldn't escape from; each time we struggled, the grip got tighter. We looked up to see who held us.

It was the witch. She must have come silently, sneaking up on us on her bike, and waited for us to come out through the gap in the trees. She had grabbed us so hard and fast that we were caught off guard. She shoved us roughly along the footpath, and through her squeaky old gate. We were hastily jostled down the overgrown, moss-covered path that led down beside the shabby old house. As we rounded the back corner of the house, we could hear a low, bone-chilling growling sound. The witch shoved us into a corner that was formed by the back wall of the house, and a broken down veranda that jutted out from the wall. As we stumbled into the corner, she shook us violently to force us to stand still.

Suddenly the source of the growling came stealthily into view. It stalked towards us, coming slowly closer and closer. It was a huge black dog, with its horrible piercing eyes fixed on us, and huge snarling teeth, bared through floppy, slobbering lips. The witch held us motionless as the monster continued to growl and snarl, as it stalked even closer. It was less than an arm's length away from us when, to our momentary relief, the creature reached the end of its chain. It swung in a side-stepping arc to the left, then to the right as it strained to reach us. It was growling furiously, gagging itself as the chain pulled hard on the collar around its neck. We were trapped in the corner by the dog, with its ability to swing sideways blocking each corner. It was so close, with its horrible eyes constantly fixed on us, that we could smell its vile, steamy breath.

The witch disappeared hastily into the house, leaving us captives of the dog. Wingnut still had hold of the windshield, so he cautiously manoeuvred it in front of us both, to create a barrier between us and the dog, which might provide us some protection for a minute or two, if the dog's tight chain should break.

It seemed like an eternity, as we stood shoulder to shoulder, backed into the corner of the house and huddled behind the old motorcycle windshield. We dared not make any sudden moves, as the horrible dog paced from side to side in a relentless, futile attempt to reach us.

As we stood captive, our eyes roamed the backyard of the house. There was no sunlight, except for fleeting glimmers of light darting through the overgrown trees, as they moved lazily in the breeze. At one time, there must have been a regular back yard here, with a lawn and a garden, but now the grass was long, and the weeds were high and gone to seed. Our minds raced as we tried to think what might happen next. I had images of Hansel and Gretel, and right now, the witch was preparing a huge pot in which to cook two little boys.

The door clicked, followed by heavy footsteps, and the witch appeared on the veranda. She had changed her clothes. Her black hat was gone, and the full-length, black dress had been replaced by grey slacks and a dark brown man's shirt.

Wingnut whispered in my ear, "She's changed into her work clothes."

"Yeah," I replied, "it doesn't look too good for us."

"What are you doing here?" she yelled, scaring our already scared selves out of our wits.

"We snuck into your place to steal this old motorbike windshield," I stammered timidly.

"Why didn't you come and ask for it, or offer to pay for it?" she asked firmly.

"We just thought that nobody would notice if we took it," I replied.

"Well, you're wrong," she screeched, "I'm going to call the police and tell them to come and arrest two trespassing thieves."

My recent life flashed before my eyes. I had lied to my mom, I had gone places and didn't tell her, I had already stolen grapes and trespassed on the Scotts' property, and now my criminal career was really being kicked off in fine style—being arrested by the police. I'm only ten years old. My panicking brain rationalized that it would probably be better than being eaten by a witch.

"Please don't call the police!" Wingnut pleaded. "My mom will kill me."

"And my dad will kill me," I added.

"Well you should have thought about that before you decided to sneak in here and steal my property," the witch answered angrily.

"Perhaps we could do some work for you to make up for it," Wingnut suggested nervously.

"What do you mean, work? What kind of work?" the witch demanded.

"Well, your yard is quite a mess, perhaps we could clean it up a bit for you."

"Quite a mess!" the witch yelled at the top of her lungs, scaring us half to death, and setting the horrible dog into a barking fit.

"Quite a mess!" she yelled again. "I'll tell you who's in quite a mess—it's two little boys caught trespassing and stealing, that's who is in quite a mess," she bellowed.

Suddenly the witch turned even paler than she already was, the angry expression slipped from her face, which rapidly turned slack, and her eyes rolled backwards in her eye sockets. Wingnut and I stood transfixed, watching the witch teeter and sway on the spot. We could feel the colour drain from our faces, as thoughts of her conjuring up a nasty spell to hurl upon us danced through our heads. Her arms went lifeless by her sides, as her knees began to oscillate from side to side. She collapsed in a heap, like a string puppet with severed strings, onto the faded boards of the veranda, and lay there like a corpse.

A cold chill bristled the hairs on the back of my neck, and a cold sweat rippled over my body as I shuddered in horror.

We clutched each other as we realized that we were now trapped between a slobbering mad dog and a dead witch.

Our instinct to make a run for it hit us both at the same time, driven by fear, horror, and danger. We looked for an avenue of escape—not past the mad dog and not past the dead person—so we picked our way along the side of the veranda, keeping out of reach of the dog. We were brushing up against the veranda handrail, only inches away from the motionless body. We moved in little side steps, wide-eyed, with racing hearts. A pale, clammy hand shot through the rungs of the handrail and clasped itself onto the shoulder of Wingnut's shirt.

"Ahhh!" Wingnut yelled, freezing me with terror to the spot by his side where I stood.

"Help me!" croaked the weak voice that came from the now stirring body. "Come and help me!" Wingnut and I looked into each other's faces for reassurance, as the witch sat up and softly beckoned us to her. We obeyed, and she directed us each to take one of her arms and help her into a nearby chair. The colour returned to her pale face as she thanked us.

"Could you fetch me a glass of water from the kitchen?" she asked politely. "There is a clean glass next to the sink." I obediently opened the door, walked into the kitchen and looked around for the sink. The inside of the house was a huge contrast to its outside appearance.

It was clean, neat, and tidy, and it looked way too nice for a witch's house! I didn't see any cages with fattening children in them, or black crows perched on a broomstick or anything. I found the glass, filled it with cold tap water, and dutifully delivered it to the veranda.

Wingnut fetched a cushion and placed it behind her back as I handed her the glass of water, which she drank without stopping.

"Where do you live?" she asked, as she dabbed little droplets of water from the side of her mouth with the long sleeve of her shirt. We formally introduced ourselves, and told her where we lived.

"We'll rake up all the dead leaves and cut your grass for you," Wingnut offered desperately.

"Well that would be very nice. By the way, my name is Mrs. Lavine. I have lived in this house for many years. My husband and I moved here when we were newlyweds. This house was quite beautiful in those days, and the garden was a showpiece. Unfortunately my husband was called away to fight in the war, and he was killed in France in 1943.

"Before he left for the war, we stored a lot of our stuff beside the house, so that we could use it all again when he returned. That's his motorcycle still parked there. He only had it a year before he covered it up and left it.

"After I heard that he had been killed, I got very sick and spent many months in the house alone, looking after myself the best I could. I never really recovered, and the illness left me quite frail, weak, and prone to fainting spells, as you have seen. After spending many years inside, I developed an acute sensitivity to the sun. The only time I ever ventured out was in the early evening, when the sun was setting, to go to the grocery store to buy food and necessities while everyone else was eating dinner with their families. If I go at any other time, I have to cover myself from head to foot to protect myself from the sun."

"We thought you were a witch," Wingnut stated respectfully, not wishing to set her off into a rage. She smiled slightly and said,

"Yes, I expect I do look a little like that I suppose. Did I frighten you?"

"Yes," we both chimed a jinx again.

"But not as much as your dog," Wingnut added.

"He's really a big softie," she confessed. "He's no longer used to people, so he gets very excited. He would probably love to play with you."

"Yeah, play with us until were dead, then eat us," Wingnut added nervously.

"Oh no!" Mrs. Lavine corrected, "He hasn't eaten anyone for a couple of weeks. I think he's gotten over doing that," she said matter-of-factly.

Wingnut and I both looked at her suspiciously with furrowed brows, as we digested what she had said. She laughed weakly, which sent her into a coughing fit.

"I'm only kidding," she stammered, between coughs and gasps for breath. We smiled slightly, but didn't really know if she was joking or not, as the dog sat staring at us constantly, tugging at his chain and licking his chops.

The old rusty padlock on the door of the half-rotten, tilting garden shed came open on our third attempt to get a key into it. The door was bound up on the bottom corner due to the drastic lean of the roof. We both heaved on the handle until the old wooden door succumbed to the force we had exerted on it, breaking in half across the centre. The top half fell open by itself, while we dragged the bottom half reluctantly into an open position. A shaft of sunlight pierced through the overhanging trees and stabbed itself into the gloomy interior of the shed. Other slivers of light shafted through knotholes and cracks in the walls and roof. Each one illuminated the dust particles which we had stirred up at different angles, creating a crisscross of light beams, as we stared into the darkness, like two archeologists who had just opened King Tutankhamun's tomb for the first time.

As our eyes adjusted to the darkness, we found no royal treasure, just a huge assortment of garden tools, an old green wheelbarrow, a rusty steel wheel, and an assortment of saws, hammers and other hand tools hanging by nails on the wall. In the far corner, we could see the word "Dennis" through a pile of clay flowerpots and garden tool handles. We crept carefully to the back of the shed and moved the stack of clay pots to one side, and removed the long-handled garden tools from where they lay. There were hoes, shovels, rakes, spades, garden forks and brooms, which we untangled one by one, to reveal a huge, green motor mower sitting sedately in the corner of the shed.

We selected a rake each, and set about raking the entire back lawn. It was covered with many years of fallen leaves, small twigs, and branches that had come down with the wind. We were sweating with the effort, as we finally wheelbarrowed the last of the gathered leaves onto a huge pile, which we had made at the end of the property.

Mrs. Lavine called us to come to the veranda. To our surprise, she had two tall glasses filled with a red drink. On the table beside her sat a tall, slender bottle with a label that read "Ribena Black Current Syrup." We gratefully downed our cool drinks and set our glasses down on the table.

"If you come back tomorrow morning and cut the grass for me, I will give you the motorcycle windshield that you were after," Mrs. Lavine declared. We looked at each other questioningly.

"Or would you rather I call the police to give you a ride home in their police car?" A cold silence filled the air as we weighed up the options.

"Can we go now?" Wingnut asked respectfully.

"Will you come back tomorrow?" asked Mrs. Lavine, in the same tone.

"Yes, we'll come early, as we would love to have the windshield," Wingnut added enthusiastically.

"What on earth do you want it for?" she asked.

"Oh! It's for a secret project that we are working on. See you tomorrow!" Wingnut called out, as we sprinted off like a couple of scared rabbits down the path beside the house. We didn't bother to open the old gate, we just ducked our heads and darted through a gap in the bushes. We didn't stop running until we were safe in our headquarters behind the garage.

The next morning, Wingnut was knocking at our back door before I had even gotten dressed. My mom invited him in, and he joined us in our pyjamas for a breakfast of vegemite on toast, a glass of milk, and a boiled egg in an eggcup, which we spooned out of the cut-off shell with a teaspoon.

I ran to my room to get dressed, while Mom chatted with Wingnut as she cleaned off the table and started washing the dishes.

"So! What are you two monkeys up to today?" Mom asked.

"Oh, we met this lady down the street who hasn't been well lately. We're going to mow her lawn for her."

"That's nice dear," Mom said without turning her head from the task at hand. Wingnut grinned at me and elbowed me in the ribs. I elbowed him back and we both took off out the back door.

We paused at the old gate in front of Mrs. Lavine's house. Without any communication between us, we simultaneously darted to the left, and disappeared through the small gap in the trees that we had used yesterday. It felt very strange, walking cautiously down the little path beside the house of our own free will, when just yesterday, we had feared for our lives at the hands of an angry witch. We peered around the corner of the house; there was no one in sight, and no horrible dog to be seen. Suddenly there was a muffled bang from the vicinity of the old garden shed, and a movement caught our eye.

Mrs. Lavine emerged from the shed wearing a large safari hat and gray pants, with a man's shirt. She stood up to her full height, once outside the shed. In the morning light she looked like a totally different person than the one who had terrified us yesterday.

She looked pleasant and smiled kindly at us as we approached.

"I filled this can with petrol," she declared, holding a small, red, metal jerry can triumphantly at arm's length.

"Let's see if we can get this old mower started. It's been many years since it was last used—I hope it's still working," she said, as she disappeared back into the darkness of the shed. She began handing things to us through the slanted doorway, to clear a path for the extraction of the entombed mower.

Wingnut gathered up an armful of garden tools and carried them around to the back of the shed, in order to stack them up against the back wall.

He screamed in fear as he dropped his burden with a sudden crash. He clasped his arms over his head in protection as the huge dog came charging at a full run, from around the back corner of the shed. Plumes of light dust puffed up from the ground, as the massive, black paws pounded their galloping way toward him.

He seemed frozen to the spot as the dog skidded to a halt in front of him, with its huge, slobbering mouth flapping with the motion. The dog sprang up at Wingnut, standing on its hind legs and slamming its two massive, black front paws onto both of his shoulders. The force and fright knocked Wingnut right off his feet. The dog rode him to the ground, pinning him with both front paws still on his shoulders. Wingnut kicked and screamed as he felt the dog lungeing its slobbering, drooling mouth at his throat.

Mrs. Lavine raced to his assistance, grabbing the dog's large collar with both hands. She tried to heave the dog's massive head away from Wingnut, who was gagging and spitting frantically, as the dog licked and drooled all over his face with its huge lips slithering about in their own spit.

"I think you've made a new friend," Mrs. Lavine grunted, as she exerted herself once again to remove the excited dog from Wingnut's face. She fastened the quivering dog to its chain, and offered Wingnut a cleaning rag from her pants pocket to wipe the shiny slobber from his face. He had already removed most of it with the sleeve of his shirt, as he continued to cough and spit, in an effort to remove the remnants from his mouth.

"He's really excited to have some company. I hope he didn't frighten you," she said as she wiped off the leftover slimy bits that Wingnut's sleeve had missed.

"Frightened!" Wingnut blurted out. "Frightened! Why would I be frightened? Being flattened by a monster dog twice my size, having my entire head sucked clean like a sucker on a stick—oh no, that happens to me every day. I'm used to it," Wingnut yelled mockingly.

Mrs. Lavine approached him and closely examined his still-moist face.

"I think it's improved your complexion," she said quietly.

Wingnut's mood changed immediately, as we all burst out laughing. The dog tugged on its chain, longing for another suck on Wingnut's lollipop head.

The old green mower was rolled sedately out into the sunlight, and parked ceremoniously in front of the shed. We walked around it several times—it was an impressive machine. It had no wheels, just a large metal roller in the back, and a spiral-shaped, rotating cutting blade in the front, tucked in behind the huge, green, metal grass-catcher, which had the word "Dennis" proudly displayed across its front.

"This was the best lawn mower money could buy when we bought it," Mrs. Lavine informed us. "It's the same one that the Queen has, to mow the lawns at Windsor Castle," she added.

The long since evaporated fuel was replenished with the fresh petrol. Mrs. Lavine drew the long, slender oil dipstick from its tubular sleeve and examined the level. It was still up to the upper graduation mark. Wingnut found the large, black knob marked "choke" and pulled it out until it stopped. Mrs. Lavine explained the controls to us, demonstrating which lever drove the blades, and which lever drove the roller to make it go forward.

She searched around the motor until she found the small primer lever, attached to the side of the carburetor. She pumped it up and down several times, and stood back as she said,

"OK boys let's try it." I took hold of the large crank handle, and heaved on it with all my might. Nothing happened. I pulled harder, and still nothing.

"Put your foot right there, and really heave on it," said Mrs. Lavine, indicating the appropriate foot placement spot. With both hands clasped tightly on the handle, standing on one leg with the other braced against the body of the mower, I heaved again with all my might. The huge motor turned over twice.

After three more attempts, each time the technique improving, the motor coughed with a hint of life and then instantly died. I rested from the exertion as Wingnut strained with all his shiny-faced might, and managed to get another three or four splutters. We traded places once again, and after several more strenuous attempts, the majestic old mower coughed and sputtered into life. It chugged desperately, belching smoke in huge puffs from the muffler, where four large spiders came frantically crawling from their unfortunate hiding place. The mower shook and vibrated, giving signs of snuffing itself out, until Mrs. Lavine pushed the black choke knob back in. The motor began to settle down into a smooth, rhythmic chug, as the mighty old machine pulsed with long lost life.

Runaway mower

Wingnut shoved forward the lever that operated the cutting blades. They sprang into life instantly, grating and grinding for a few seconds as the fine layer of rust on the cutting edges wore itself off. They then seemed to sing with a finely-tuned ring, as they sheared in unison over the cutting bar that they had once been finely adjusted to, by caring and knowledgeable hands. The mower's handle and controls were high on Wingnut's chest. He reached up and shut off the cutting blades, then activated the drive roller lever.

The old Dennis lunged forward immediately, and motored off across the scruffy, overgrown lawn, with Wingnut trotting behind it, frantically grasping at the levers in an attempt to stop it. The mower chugged at jogging speed, seemingly thrilled to finally be free and moving again after its years of solitary confinement. Wingnut caught up with it, as it plowed through the large pile of leaves that we had just raked the day before. The mower never changed its pitch, as it parted the pile of leaves like Moses at the Red Sea. Leaves spewed in all directions and the mower never slowed or wavered in any way, as it bulldozed its way through the huge pile and went crashing through the old wooden fence at the back of the yard. The dog barked excitedly at the commotion, until the mower finally came to a standstill in a pile of rubble and broken boards, stopped not by a stalled engine, but simply by loss of traction. The roller rode up onto some slippery remnants of the fence, and the motor still chugged faithfully away, the drive roller spinning in place, seemingly looking for some purchase so it could continue on its joyous, boisterous outing.

We took turns in taming the wild mower. Once we had it broken in, it was more than willing to respond to our commands, after we had mastered all the levers and controls. We ran the mighty Dennis up and down the scruffy lawn, leaving straight, groomed paths in its wake. We groomed the entire back lawn and only had to empty the massive catcher once. We parked the Dennis in the shed when we were done, and Mrs. Lavine presented us with the windshield, which she had cleaned and polished. We promised that we would come back and mow the grass in the front next weekend, and we marched off and disappeared through the gap in the bushes, with the hard-earned fruit of our labor finally in our hands.

In the dim light of the garage, we stood side by side in silence, looking at the armoured bike we had created. We held the prized windshield up onto the front, where we thought it should go.

"It doesn't fit. There's nothing to attach it to." We placed it face-up on the floor in disappointment, and stood silently looking at it with staring, unblinking eyes. Without saying it, we both realized that fatigue had set in from our day with the Dennis.

We opened up the front door of the garage and wheeled the bike around to our headquarters in the back, placing the windshield inside and covering it with a piece of old potato sack that we had used to sit on.

CHAPTER 13

The dark green Austin A40 purred along quietly, as Mom drove sedately along the avenue that ran past the school. She had turned right at the end of the street, and sped up a little as the road left the houses behind, opening up into grassy fields on the left, and a wide, slow-moving, weed-filled river on the right. I watched as the trees, bushes, fences, and little bridges flashed by and disappeared behind us.

"How deep is the water in the river?" I asked, interrupting my mom's thoughts as she peered over the steering wheel into the distance ahead of us.

"It's not a river dear. It's a manmade canal that the early settlers built about 80 years ago. They had planned to build the canal all the way from the estuary into the centre of the city, so that goods and merchandise could be transported by barge into a central market place there. However, only one year after the construction of the canal had begun another group of engineers and businessmen began to build a railway line into the city, only four miles away. Of course the railroad was completed first, and the canal project was abandoned. This part of it is the actual size that the completed canal would have been. It only goes a few miles, and then it turns into a storm water drain, which goes under our street and continues all the way into town, where it connects with a river there. If it rains a lot, most of the city's rain gutters empty into the river, and in turn, into the drain, which carries all the excess water to the estuary, where it is controlled by some floodgates, which we will be passing shortly. The city hasn't flooded from a lengthy rainstorm for years, as the drain seems to carry the water away quite well. But when it hasn't rained for a long time, the drain gets a little stagnant and small animals fall into it from time to time."

"Yeah I know," I said confidently.

As we drove alongside the canal, I could see from the car window that the water didn't flow very fast; in fact, the canal was full of waterweed and lily pads that formed small islands on top of the water. There was an assortment of ducks and wild swamp birds swimming sedately in the calm grey water. The road took a sharp right turn; the canal ended abruptly and seemed to disappear into a culvert that passed under the road. On the other side of the road there was a vast expanse of water that Mom described as an inlet to the sea that was surrounded by land, and which was a mixture of seawater and river water. She said that the estuary rose and fell with the tides, and was fed and drained of water through a narrow gap that led out to the sea.

"That's where we are going," she said without taking her eyes off the road. "I'm going to do a painting of a unique rock formation that is located just a short distance from the mouth of the estuary. You can play on the beach while I paint."

"Can I go for a swim when we get there?" I asked.

"Oh no dear, you can never swim there. The tide creates an extremely strong current as it rushes through the narrow inlet; many people have drowned or gone missing. Even motor boats can't go against the current, and dozens of small boats have been swept out to sea over the years. Many people sail their small yachts and sailboats on the estuary at high tide. They all know to keep well away from the inlet when the tide starts to go out."

"Where are the flood gates?" I asked casually.

"We just passed them. They're right at the end of the road where the canal ends."

"Can we go back and see them?" I blurted out excitedly.

"No dear. Perhaps on the way back we can take a look." I sunk back into my seat; I had missed my only chance to see the floodgates. I would have loved to tell Wingnut all about them. I stared at the floor in disappointment, until I was shaken out of my trance by the car being bumped and jolted as Mom steered it down a narrow, rutted dirt track, toward the beach, where we lurched to a stop. As the dust settled around us, I could see the large rock formation that Mom intended to paint. She gathered up an armful of stuff from the back seat, handed me her wooden easel, and walked off with a determined stride into the sand dunes. She circled around several times until she found a satisfactorily sheltered spot. She set herself up with a small table on which she laid out her tubes of paint and her brushes. She had a folding chair, a blanket, a picnic basket and a thermos of tea. The rock formation was framed by low sand dunes, which gave it the appearance of being grander than it actually was. She placed her wide-brimmed straw hat on her head, and tied the two ribbons under her chin to secure it against the slight, warm breeze.

I found a banana in the picnic basket, and ate it as I watched her studying the rock and carefully sketching what she saw onto the white canvas, with a stick of willow charcoal.

I stuck another banana in my pocket like a gun in a holster, and swaggered off through the sand dunes like John Wayne in the Texas desert. The dunes soon opened up onto a huge, gray, deserted sandy beach. The waves crashed loudly as they disintegrated on the beach, washing up onto the hard, flat sand with a soothing, swishing sound. Little islands of foam danced and jiggled in the wind, while further out, the tips of the waves were thrashed white in the churning water, with streams of spray whipping off their crests in the wind.

The tide was going out and from where I stood, I could see the swirling, turbulent current forcing its way mercilessly into the opposing surf. I spotted a piece of driftwood trapped in the current. It was moving past me, bobbing and dipping as it was sucked along in the turbulence. I began to follow it along the shore; it was moving as fast as I could walk. Suddenly, my eyes were distracted by a flashing movement right out in the middle of the river-like current. I strained to search for it, looking left and right to detect another movement amid the turbulence. Suddenly there it was again, then again, and again. It was evident that I was seeing a rather large fish darting about in the mouth of the estuary, feeding on smaller fish that were caught in the strong current.

I lost sight of the driftwood I was following, as it was sucked under by the ferocious undertow that was created when the two masses of water collided. As I turned to head off along the beach, I was startled by a loud splash just a short distance behind me.

I froze to the spot momentarily, and then spun around on the balls of my feet just in time to see a huge, grey mass lunge up from the depths of the churning current. White spray streaked off its grey body as it broke the surface. Its massive mouth was splayed open and seawater gushed out from the sides, as the huge, white rows of teeth clenched instantly shut on a mouthful of struggling fish.

The huge shark was feeding ravenously on the bounty of food that appeared daily at this spot. I watched excitedly as I saw the shark break the surface once more and crash back into the water with a splash that I could hear over the noise of the waves on the beach and the wind in my ears.

Seagulls trotted nervously, constantly looking over their shoulders as I walked down the broad expanse of beach, with the wind whipping and tugging on my shirt and tousling my hair. I found the remains of an old fishing net half buried in the sand. On the end of it there was a bright orange ball of cork, which was rolling back and forth on its tether in the wind.

I knelt down in the sand and untied the knot that held it in place. Once it had come free, I held it in my hand as I ran at full speed across the beach and hurled the float into the surf as hard as I could. I watched it disappear and reappear as it bobbed about freely in the churning water.

I headed back across the beach toward the sand dunes. I soon found my way blocked by a large pool of water, right in the middle of the beach. I decided to simply wade across it but soon discovered that it was incredibly deep. I stood for a while, peering into the water, and clearly saw that it was very deep indeed, and extremely still and clear. A passing cloud blocked the sun momentarily, and as it passed I saw something moving in the bottom of the tidal pool. I executed a John Wayne, quick draw of the banana, and took a few imaginary shots at the large crayfish that had been trapped in the pool by the receding tide.

Peeling the banana as I walked back to the spot where I'd seen the old fishing net, I was struck by the idea of trying to catch the crayfish.

I folded the flaps of the banana peel back into place and stuffed the banana back into my pocket, as I knelt to dig up a fairly long length of fishing net cord. I managed to find several others and tied them all together end to end until I had quite a long piece. I rolled it all up and hung it over my arm, as I set about eating the now-browning banana. I had finished it by the time I arrived back at the tidal pool, where I peered into the depths to relocate the lone crayfish. I tied a misshaped stone onto the end of the cord and wrapped the stone in the banana peel and tied it in place with some short remnants of cord that I had in my pocket.

I tossed the wrapped stone out into the centre of the deep pool, and watched it as it sank to the bottom. I missed my target, so I pulled in the cord and threw it again and again until finally it landed over the top of the sluggish crayfish. I slowly dragged the banana-wrapped stone across the bottom of the pool, until it came in contact with the crayfish. I left it still, as he slowly wrapped his claws about the stone and began nibbling at the banana peel.

I moved it a little, and he clung on to it tighter, so I began to slowly reel in the cord, dragging the crayfish, still clinging onto his little prize, right across the bottom of the pool and up to the surface. He began to panic as his body came clear of the water, but it was too late. He was already stranded on the beach.

"Ha! What a catch I've just made. Wait till Mom sees this—no fishing rod, no hook, no bait. Nothing except a stone and a banana peel."

I tied up the struggling crayfish with the cord, and set off up the beach in the direction I had come.

The shadow I cast on the wet sand was long. I stared at it as I walked, watching it wave and flicker as it passed over the regular ripples in the sand. I amused myself by jumping in the air and dancing about, trying to trick the shadow, as its feet disconnected from my own only to match up again when I landed.

I laughed out loud to myself as I put the crayfish on my head and strutted about, doing my best "rich lady in a fancy hat" impression. I turned and posed sideways with the crayfish held in both hands at my waist, as if I was taking a pee. I thrust out my pelvis as I leaned back to admire the huge bulge that my shadow seemed to have in his pants.

"What on earth are you doing?" The loud, shrill voice startled me instantly back to reality. I straightened up immediately, dropping the crayfish on my foot in fright. The sharp spines pierced into the top of my foot, making me yelp with pain. I clutched my foot in both hands as I hopped about in circles on one leg, trying to soothe the pain.

"Stop that fooling about immediately. Where have you been? I've been looking for you everywhere. I thought you had fallen into the estuary and been swept out to sea."

"I caught a crayfish," I called out, forgetting my foot as I brandished my catch at arm's length in the air and ran up the sand dune to where Mom had established a lookout.

"Throw that thing away," she scolded, "you can't eat stuff that has been washed up on the beach."

"I caught it in a pool," I said defensively. "Look, it's still alive."

"You mean it's fresh?" Mom asked.

"Yes," I replied as she examined it closely.

The car was packed and ready to go. It was obvious that Mom had waited for me for quite a while, and since I hadn't been swept out to sea and drowned, I might have been severely reprimanded if it weren't for the crayfish peace offering. Mom listened intently as I gave a step-by-step account of how I caught the crayfish. She pulled the car into a parking stall, went into a bakery and returned with a freshly baked loaf of bread that was still hot from the oven. As soon as we got home, the two of us sat down and ate the freshly cooked crayfish with fresh, buttered bread.

CHAPTER 14

I was already in our headquarters, sitting on a box studying the Operation Payback sketch that I had made, when Wingnut pulled back the flap and came in to sit opposite me at our makeshift table. We sat in silence, staring at the map of the street that we had made, not knowing quite where to begin.

Wingnut sneezed hard, three times in a row, into his hands. His face turned red with the effort and force of his sneezes. As he began to recover, he quickly glanced into his hand to see what he had caught, and just as quickly wiped it onto his pants as he nonchalantly gazed up, as if he were suddenly attracted to something moving on the ceiling. What the pants didn't remove was encouraged to disappear onto the front of his shirt with two quick strokes of his hand, performed so smoothly they nearly avoided detection. It was obvious that he had practiced this manoeuvre many times.

We wheeled the bike into the garage, and soon realized that we couldn't get onto the bike because we had completely boxed it in. We removed four of the horizontal wooden slats from the back, and made a small door of wire mesh, just big enough to climb through. While I tried out the seating position, Wingnut came in with the windshield and held it in front of the box that we had built. As I held the bike steady, he attempted to size it up, to see how we could actually attach it to the front of the box. He held it out in front of himself with both hands, as he positioned it this way and that, to see how it would fit.

A sneeze blasted from his nose and mouth which made his head bob forward violently, as though he had been hit in the back of the head with a bat. Another sneeze blasted out uncontrollably, but Wingnut's hand was not free to do his casual "wipe it on the pants trick," so the windshield was splattered with spit and snot. Wingnut staggered like a drunk as another sneeze wracked his body. He crashed into the bike and it began to topple over. I put out my foot to stop it, but it slipped on the gritty floor. Wingnut lost his balance as the whole thing keeled over with a mighty crash, with me inside and Wingnut sprawled face-first into the windshield. His face had smeared the remnants of his sneeze attack from one side of it to the other. He lay there in disbelief and frustration as the dust settled around us. The front top corner had snapped off during the fall as it struck the box that we had used to sit on. As Wingnut wiped his face with his sleeve like a cat having a wash, I climbed out the bottom of the box to survey the damage.

The corner had snapped off on an angle from the top cross brace which we had put in for strength, right down to the lower frame we had built to nail the bottom of the plywood to. It gave the whole thing a racy, streamlined look. While the box was on its side, we took the saw and cut off the opposite corner to match. Wingnut washed the inside of the windshield with the garden hose, and it was an easy matter to now fix it into place with two screws at the bottom, and a piece of wire across the top. The armoured bike was now complete. It looked fantastic!

Armoured bike

We raced to fling the garage doors open. Wingnut held the bike upright as I crawled in through the flap in the back, climbed over the back wheel, and assumed the riding position. Wingnut wheeled our masterpiece out into the sunlight, I began to pedal, and the armoured bike picked up speed. An excited "Yahoo!" bellowed out, as I realized I could pedal, I could steer, and I could see.

The narrow slots in the sides were at just the right height for me to see out, so down the street I went. Wingnut stood and watched with his arms folded in front of him in a stance of proud admiration and satisfaction.

The word had spread. The news of Operation Payback had reached brothers, sisters, neighbours and friends. Our armoured bike was the centre of attraction at our Wednesday meeting in the park.

The tall skinny girl had led about thirty kids to the centre of the park. They all sat on the ground and quietly listened as I explained the plan for Operation Payback, in intimate detail.

The date was set for Saturday, right after the school fair, which would end at 2 pm.

The circle of kids crammed in closer and closer as I divulged the secret details of the operation. They all studied the map I had drawn, and divided themselves into three groups. They listened intently as I explained that we should all leave the fair at exactly one o'clock, and ride to our designated ambush positions.

"Group one of course, to gather out of sight, down street number one. Group two will have to ride around to the back of the park, and position themselves out of sight in street number two, and group three must gather in behind the gate of the tennis courts.

"At two o'clock, she will . . ."

"The name's Samantha," the tall girl interrupted.

"At two o'clock, 'Samantha' will ride past the Shulaks at high speed, and hurl a water balloon over their fence, then speed away before they have a chance to react. This should rile them up enough to draw them out into the open. I will follow on the armoured bike and ride slowly past the Shulaks, who won't be able to resist coming out onto the road to attack me.

"The plan is to entice the Shulaks across the avenue and out into the open area where we have all been attacked by them before. Once they reach the tree with Wingnut's sock in it, all three groups must come out of hiding, and we will surround them from three sides and let them have it.

"Be sure to bring plenty of choice ammo, but no clods of dirt or stones, just stuff that's firm enough to throw, but will burst and splatter well on impact."

The excitement was contagious, as it boiled over into a communal cheer. Samantha led a pledge of secrecy, and it was sworn to by all. If the secret were to become broken, Operation Payback would be ruined. We must keep it strictly to ourselves. No adults or little children must know.

We took turns riding the armoured bike up and down the street. Each time there was a small change to be made, or we modified something a little, but mostly it was just plain fun, especially all the strange looks we got from people. It was a new sensation to be able to see out, but nobody could really see in.

As Wingnut was taking the bike for a spin, the wind picked up suddenly and propelled him down the street at an alarming rate. I could see him disappearing into the distance, wobbling slightly as he went. The wind had caught the bodywork that we'd built and Wingnut was sailing. He had stopped pedaling and was frantically hauling on the brakes in an effort to stop before he reached the end of the street and careened out into the traffic, which was crossing in front of him. The brake rubbers became hot with friction and began to create a juddering squeal. Suddenly the small rectangular rubber pads became so hot they softened and popped out of the sockets they were crimped into. Wingnut began to accelerate, and panic filled his chest as he realized that he had no brakes. He sped out of control and flashed past the stop sign at the end of the street, hurtling into the passing traffic flow. Three cars swerved violently, missing Wingnut by a hair's breadth; others jammed on their brakes, leaving black skid marks on the road as the wheels locked and smoked to a halt. Wingnut was about to crash head-first into a low stone wall that bordered a small park. He quickly spotted a narrow path that led through a gateless access opening, and managed to lean the speeding bike just enough to steer it masterfully through the gap. The wind hurled him forward like a sailboat in a gale. He bumped violently over a small curb and wobbled uncontrollably as he realized he was on the slippery grass, heading straight for the small pond in the centre of the park. He threw his weight over, in an attempt to avoid the water, but his wheels slid on the grass and he plunged sideways into the pond.

Crash in the pond

Spectators gathered as Wingnut thrashed about inside the armoured bike, trying desperately to get out. Fortunately, the pond was only deep enough to half submerge the bike, and once he had wiggled out, he was only knee-deep in water. An elderly man helped Wingnut haul the bike out of the pond and stand it upright. Wingnut had been blown to the end of the street so fast that he was already trying to balance the bike and push it against the wind towards home by the time I got there.

Leaves, litter, and dust swirled about us, flying, tumbling, and turning off into the distance, as Wingnut and I strained to keep the bike upright, as we forced it into the buffeting wind. With Wingnut on one side, and me on the other, we wrestled and pushed the bike all the way home. We had cleared out most of the junk beside the garage to create a perfect parking spot. The bike, with all its bodywork, slid neatly into the space and we were able to pile an assortment of loose stuff in behind it to hide it from view.

We slipped into our headquarters A-frame, and rested from our efforts in silence, as the wind outside tugged and rattled on the makeshift structure.

"What if it's windy like this on Saturday?" Wingnut asked.

"Well I suppose it will have to be plan B."

"What's plan B?" Wingnut asked seriously.

"Well, we'll dress you up like a girl, then you'll walk past the Shulaks, wiggle your eyebrows at them and throw kisses. When they come out to kiss you, then we'll get them."

"What!" Wingnut yelled. "I'm not dressing up as a girl, and I'm certainly not throwing kisses to them." I burst out laughing and Wingnut punched me on the shoulder in frustration. I began to make kissy gestures with my lips, and teased him with winks and wiggly eyebrows. He came at me, to punch me on the shoulder again, but I slipped through the door flap and ran away, with Wingnut in hot pursuit. I darted through the gap in the poplar hedge and sprinted through the long grass, down the narrow track which we had worn across the front of old Mac's house. Wingnut caught up to me when I stopped to unhook my pants that had become snagged on the barbed wire, as I climbed over the rail on the fence that crossed the drain. Wingnut scrambled over with ease and we were now out onto the street and the chase was forgotten.

"Let's go to the park and see what it's like when it's really windy," Wingnut said excitedly. Nothing more was said as we ran across the road, climbed the fence on the other side, and ran down the track between the drain and the little ditch. Wingnut's secret shortcut soon led us to the back of the park.

When we emerged from the shelter of the prickly hedge, the wind tugged and flapped our shirts as we walked, bent into the strong wind, across the park where we had been attacked by the magpies. That day had been hot and still, but today everything was moving, leaves were tumbling and racing each other across the park, and the trees seemed to be egging them on, as they swayed and waved in unison. We reached the other side of the park and stood at the base of the gigantic trees that grew in a row across the front of the park, facing the avenue. Their trunks were so big that four kids wrapped around them with their arms outstretched could barely reach all the way around.

We looked across the avenue from where we stood, and we could see the Shulaks' house in the distance.

"I wonder if they're home," I said to Wingnut casually.

"I wonder," said Wingnut. "Let's climb up to the top of these huge trees and look down, right into their front yard. You take that one, I'll take this one, and we will see if we can spy on them from the top of the trees."

CHAPTER 15

The giant tree trunks splayed out at the bottom, where they spread to form their roots. It was an easy matter to climb the rough bark to reach the first branches of the massive trees. Our rubber gumboots provided excellent grip as we progressed, branch by branch up the straight, towering trees, getting higher and higher. We progressed upward by reaching up for the next branch, as we systematically spiraled our way towards the top. Our hands were covered with sticky tree gum, and our muscles burned with the effort.

We both paused for a rest. We were only about halfway up the trees, and already we could see far off into the distance, across the rooves of the neighbouring houses. The tree trunks were now considerably smaller, and the branches were more numerous, smaller in size, and much easier to grasp. We could feel the trees swaying from side to side in the wind, forcing us to hold on tightly all the time to avoid being flung out of the trees by the motion.

Higher and higher we climbed, calling out to each other from time to time for reassurance, but the howl of the wind through the branches made it impossible to hear each other any longer. Fear set in as we realized how incredibly high we were, and how pronounced the sway of the trees was. Now that we were near the top, every ounce of strength and determination was required to hold on to the now bucking trees, which were actually traveling back and forth, about the length of a car garage, as they violently swayed through their waving arcs. The whipping action at the end of each sway, as it changed direction, was a tremendous force to fight against. Our arms wrapped around the trunks, with our hands clasped tight on the other side. We were trapped by the motion, as any attempt to let go of the trunks to climb down would send us flying like a bug being flicked off the end of a stick. The huge back and forth motion was sickening, as we clung like tiny insects waving through the air. I thought of an old sailing ship lookout man, sitting in the crow's nest at the top of the mast during a storm.

Tree climbing encounter

I glanced over to Wingnut's tree. He was hugging the tree trunk with one arm, with his cheek pressed hard against it, as he frantically gestured with his other hand, pointing urgently toward the ground. I realized that he was indicating that we must try to get down. I could sense that the wind was getting even stronger, and the swaying more violent. I began to sweat with fear, as I forced myself to let one hand free so I could lower my body down to the branch below me. I released one foot and lowered myself as I grappled in the air below me with the other, searching for a lower branch to step down to. I froze in place, hanging on with all my strength, as the tree whipped to the end of its stroke and flicked back in the other direction. My free leg dangled and whipped about also, my toe touched something below me, and I searched frantically, feeling my way with my dangling leg. My toe touched it again. I dabbed about with my foot, not daring to look down. I was stretched out full-length, with my left knee at my chin, and my right leg fully extended below me. I was in a very unstable position. As the tree whipped back in the opposite direction, my left leg was jerked free with the force of the motion. I was left dangling with my legs frantically kicking about, as my arms strained to catch hold of the branch above me.

Fear ripped through my chest and stung its way through my brain, as I realized that there was no way I would survive the next whip of the tree. My mind's eye created instant visions of myself being ripped from the tree and tumbling end over end, down through the branches of the tree, until I plunged into the ground in a mangled mess.

My shin crashed into something solid. I winced with eye-watering pain, as I drew my leg up in a convulsion of agony. My leg came up over what I had hit and my gumboots found some purchase on the rough bark of the branch below me. I realized that I was actually hanging with my feet down past the branch that would save me from certain mutilation.

I was stable again, and I had survived another whip of the violently swaying tree. Now there was an opportunity to look down, to see where I should step next. Bit by bit, minute by minute, I made my way down. The tree branches became bigger and bigger, and the sway less and less, as I slowly but surely made my way down. My hands were sore, my arms ached, and I had a goose egg on my shin. If it weren't for my gumboots, I'm sure I would have been cut and bleeding.

Wingnut and I emerged from the branches at the bottom of the tree at nearly the same time. We dropped to the ground and stood slumped over with exhaustion, breathing heavily from our exertion.

"Wasn't that exciting?" Wingnut panted sarcastically. "Perhaps we could do it again sometime."

"Yeah, perhaps on a calm day—that would be a nice change."

Wingnut burst out laughing, causing some of the pine needles and tree pollen to fall from his littered hair. He had a big stain of tree gum on the side of his face from hugging the trunk, and his hands were nearly black with sticky sap.

He looked very different for some reason, and it wasn't just the dirty state he was in from being in the dusty tree. His ears looked really weird. They naturally stuck out quite a bit, but now they looked like inflatable water wings on the side of his head. They were bright pink, with multitudes of little white lumps all over the top edges of both of them. They were twice as thick as normal, and they stuck out at a ridiculous-looking angle.

"What?" he said, shrugging his shoulders in a questioning gesture. As he shrugged palms up, his ears wobbled stiffly in a hilarious manner. I couldn't answer him, as peals of laughter were trying to burst out from the back of my throat. I forced them back, but Wingnut's swollen ears wiggled again, and it was more than I could stand. My laughter exploded. Wingnut stared at me in wonder, as I progressed into hysterics.

"What are you laughing at?" he yelled angrily. I roared uncontrollably again, his face went red to match his ears, and this was even funnier. He yelled at me again, and both ears wobbled and jiggled which was exceedingly funny. With tears in my eyes and aching sides, I howled with laughter as Wingnut became angrier and angrier. In frustration, he rushed at me and wrestled me to the ground. I laughed even harder. He punched me in the shoulder, and the impact jarred his ears and they wobbled more than before. I couldn't catch my breath, as the gut-rolling peals burst forth. He punched me in the arm again.

"What's so funny?" he screamed at the top of his voice.

"Your ears!" I stammered. "Your ears look so hilarious." He stopped suddenly and reached up with both hands to feel his ears. His eyebrows went up, and his mouth dropped open in shock, as he felt the swelling.

"What's happened?" he yelled, as he ran his fingers frantically over his puffed up ears.

"I think you've had a reaction to the tree pollen," declared a firm voice behind us. We spun around in surprise to see Mrs. Brown, who lived on our street, standing right behind us.

"It's not nice to laugh at other people's misfortunes," she said in a stern, raised voice. "Now get yourself up off the ground this instant, and stop this foolishness. Look at the state of you both, rolling about on the ground behaving like a couple of drunken fools. Now do something useful, and help me with these bags."

She had five huge bags of groceries, one in the wicker basket on the front of her old bike, and two threaded on each side of her handle bars. She thrust two bags matter-of-factly at Wingnut, and I received the other two just as sternly. We held the heavy bags, one in each hand, as we plodded off down the road, with Mrs. Brown wheeling her bike beside us, relentlessly bombarding us with lectures about our behaviour, and how useless, lazy, and disrespectful the youth of today is. By the time we reached her house, our arms were six inches longer, and our hands were burning with pain, from the handles of the bags, cutting into them. We were nearly convinced that all we needed was a good stint in the army to straighten us out. I wanted to ask Mrs. Brown how we would go about doing that, since we were only ten, but I thought I had better not.

CHAPTER 16

The wind blew itself away during the night. The morning air was cool and fresh, and the early sunlight sparkled in the millions of droplets of dew, which hung suspended in the invisible spider webs that held them.

I pulled the armoured bike out of its hiding place beside the garage, and set about repairing the damage caused by Wingnut's sailing trip into the pond.

The most serious damage was not to the wood structure we had built, but to the brakes. We had to be able to stop.

There was a bicycle repair shop right across the avenue from our school. I ran to the house and told Mom that I was going to Wingnut's house to play.

"Before you go anywhere, I want you to go to Mrs. Trop's house and buy me two dozen eggs. Here's the money," she said as she placed the folded money into my shirt pocket. "Now be very careful bringing them home, I don't want any broken ones this time. I don't want you fooling around on your bike on the way home and breaking them like you did last time, so take your brother's bike so you can place the eggs in the saddle bag, and ride home carefully."

I headed off down the road to Mrs. Trop's house, which was right next to the drain. She had several large chicken houses on her property and she sold the eggs according to the amount the hens laid each day. The eggs were always unwashed and covered with dried chicken poop. I hated to go there, as Mr. Trop was a really scary man who was always dirty and unshaven, and his long bony face and hooked nose made him look like a desperate criminal. He never spoke, but he was always looking, just lurking around in the background, watching from the corner of his eye.

Mrs. Trop was a large, overweight woman who always wore her hair in a bun on the top of her head. She also wore dirty clothes, and a cooking apron that seemed to be perpetually splattered with a wide assortment of smeared goo and different coloured stains. I parked my brother's bike at the huge gate at the end of their gravel driveway, and crunched my way, step by step, to the back door. Creepy old Mr. Trop was feeding his fat dog near the back door. The dog was busy chewing on a whole boiled cow's heart. It was a grey gristly mass, and the attached arteries jiggled and slapped on the dog's jaws as he chewed. Mr. Trop looked up slyly, and stood staring at me with his sunken, beady eyes as I knocked on the half-open back door.

Uncomfortable minutes passed as I stood on the back step fidgeting, while old man Trop kept eyeing me, as he stalked over to an ever-running tap that was fed from an underground well. He filled a battered, filthy dish with water, and placed it in front of the dog, as Mrs. Trop's voice filtered out to me from within the house.

"Come in," she called. I hesitated on the doorstep; I didn't want to go into their house. "Come in," she called again.

I gingerly pushed the door open wide enough to peer inside. There was a room full of old boxes, old shoes, and some vegetable crates. I stepped silently into the room, looking from side to side cautiously, as I tiptoed toward the light in the doorway ahead of me. I heard a noise and stopped to listen. Someone was walking in the house. Suddenly, Mrs. Trop appeared in the doorway.

"Have you come for eggs?" she said calmly.

"Yes, two dozen," I replied bravely.

"Come in," she beckoned, as she turned to walk towards the kitchen. I followed her in. The floor was splattered from one end to the other with dried drips and spills from long ago that had never been wiped up. There were two dog food bowls in the corner, which were seething, black, with hundreds of flies. The stale air stunk with the sickening stench of boiled meat, and I visualized the huge heart that the dog had been chewing. I looked up as something above me caught my eye. There were curly, brown streamers hanging from the ceiling—dozens of them. The entire ceiling was a forest of dangling paper streamers. When I looked closer, I could see that they were all encrusted with dead flies that had been caught on their sticky glue coating, as they landed. As the flypapers filled up, they must have been replaced with new ones, and the old, fly-laden ones were simply left in place.

Mrs. Trop handed me two brown paper bags bulging with eggs. I handed her the money and headed urgently to the door, desperate to escape the stench and the fly cemetery on the ceiling. Mr. Trop was standing, stooped and motionless, outside the door as I left. He said nothing as I passed him. I could feel his cold eyes on me as I turned and walked down the driveway to the gate. I had the urge to run as fast as I could, but the valuable, fragile bags I carried forced me to walk carefully.

I gently placed the two bags of eggs into the saddlebag on the bike, and clicked the flap shut. I rode carefully, trying to avoid any bumps in the road that might jar the eggs.

As I rode up the slight slope of the bridge as it crossed the drain, I caught a glimpse of something moving in the long grass at the side of the road. It moved again. I was still on edge from my visit to the Trops' house. I swerved out onto the road, and rode across to the other side of the street; some instinct had alerted me to unknown danger. Two figures sprang from the grass. The fright of it made me pedal as fast as I could. I glanced over my shoulder—it was the Shulaks lying in ambush. I had a good head start on them as they began hurling apples at me. One hit my front wheel and the spokes shredded it to pieces on impact. One or two others hit the bike, but I realized that none had hit me. I sped past them so fast that they gave up the chase. I kept my speed up, bent over the handlebars as I swerved into our driveway, and came to a stop at the garage doors.

A huge feeling of relief came over me as I realized I was home safe and sound. I opened the saddlebag and reached in to retrieve the eggs. The bag came out in my hand in a gooey, soggy mess. One of the apples had hit the saddlebag and the eggs were all smashed, except for a few survivors, bobbing around in a deep puddle in the bottom of the saddlebag.

"Those Shulaks will pay for this," I swore under my breath, as I tipped the bike over on its side to pour the congealed, yellow-flecked mess out onto a shallow pan that I had taken from the garage and placed in the flower garden, under the kitchen window.

As the eggs globbed slowly out, I was able to catch the unbroken eggs as they slowly rolled towards the edge of the open saddlebag.

A sharp knocking sound startled me, and I nearly dropped the bike into the shimmering puddle that the broken eggs had formed.

I glanced up over my shoulder. The kitchen blinds had been raised to their full open position, and Mom was watching me through the window. She was doing a really good mime—a trapped-behind-the-glass impersonation. She waved her arms about, her eyebrows had disappeared way up under her hair, and her mouth was moving rapidly as though she was yelling. I immediately recognized the yelling impression, and the rest of the interpretation of the mime story suddenly became very clear. I assumed that the ending was not going to be good.

After Mom had finished going berserk about the broken eggs, I was sent back to the creepy Trops to get another two dozen eggs, half of which was to be paid for from my next week's pocket money.

My big brother was sent with me for protection, after I was finally permitted to explain the Shulak attack. He went into the house to get the eggs, while I waited outside. Old Man Trop was nowhere to be seen, nor was there any sign of the nasty Shulaks on the way home. We carefully carried a bag of eggs each as we walked home, chatting as we went. My brother told me that he had once gone over to the Shulaks to visit with their older sister. I was amazed to hear that the horrible Shulaks actually had a sister. He went on to tell me that when he went into their backyard to knock on the door, the yard was a shambles of busted-up stuff, and broken toys. There was no lawn or grass, just bare dirt; the two boys had destroyed everything.

He said that the Shulaks had an old galvanized tub out in the middle of the yard, half-filled with water. They had put a small puppy in it and were watching it swim around and around trying to get out. My brother had walked to the shop at the corner of the street with the Shulaks' sister, to buy an ice cream. When they returned from their walk, the two boys had taken off to do something else and the little puppy was still in the tub, dead. It had simply gotten exhausted and drowned.

Tink! There it was again, the sound that had woken me up—tink.

"What is that?" I wondered out loud, as I peeked through my blinds to see what the noise at my window was. Tink again, right in front of my face. As I squinted out into the early morning light, I saw Wingnut standing a short distance from the house among roses and peonies, tossing small pebbles at my window. I freed the latch, and gently squeaked the window open.

"What are you doing?" I whispered out into the cool morning air.

"It's Saturday—today's the day," he replied in a hushed voice.

I closed the window, fastened the latch and closed the blinds, got dressed and tiptoed through the house and out through the back door.

We ran to the back of the garage and into our operations hut. I retrieved the map I had drawn days earlier, folded it neatly and stashed it in my shirt pocket.

We rolled the armoured bike from its hiding place, and wheeled it around the garage, down the driveway, and out onto the street.

"I forgot something," I blurted. I left Wingnut holding the bike as I sprinted down the driveway, dashed into the garage, and returned with a weighty, plastic shopping bag, knotted at the top.

I climbed through the back of the bike body and rode off down the street, with Wingnut jogging alongside. We turned onto the tree-lined avenue, and headed towards our school. The armoured bike was quite easy to pedal, despite the extra weight. We arrived at the tennis courts and Wingnut gestured for me to stop. I applied both brakes. Nothing! Wingnut sprinted after me, grabbed the back of the bike and wrestled me to a stop.

"I forgot to fix the brakes," I yelled in anger and frustration. "Mom sent me to creepy Trops' to buy eggs, just as I was about to go get new brake rubbers," I explained in a ground-stomping tantrum.

"Well it's too late now. Let's stash the bike in here until one o'clock," Wingnut said matter-of-factly, as he gestured toward the long narrow space that was walled in by the back of the tennis court fence. We wheeled the armoured bike into the shady, concealed space. At the far end, there was a pile of medium-sized cardboard boxes, all neatly stacked with their top flaps interleaved, to keep them closed.

"What are all those?" I asked.

"Ammo," Wingnut replied briskly. "I have been stacking them here all week."

Wingnut and I jogged non-stop down the secret shortcut, leaving the armoured bike well hidden behind the tennis courts. We split up in the direction of our respective houses without a word, except for a casual "See ya at the fair."

CHAPTER 17

The kettle whistled urgently, as I lay on my bed, fully dressed from our early morning rendezvous. The smell of bacon cooking reached my nostrils, then it was toast. That was my cue to appear in the kitchen, pretending to rub the sleep from my eyes.

The gigantic cake Mom had baked, at the cost of four dozen eggs, sat on the kitchen table. It was iced and sliced, ready to go to the school fair.

"I want you to hold the cake on your lap," Mom declared as she headed me off in the direction of the car parked in the garage.

"I'm going to walk to the fair with Wingnut," I blathered desperately, as I saw all our plans for Operation Payback disappearing out the window, at the thought of having to wait forever for Mom to finish up at the fair, then drive me home in the car.

"Well, you're not! You can come with me, and hold onto the cake." Cold panic darted about in my brain, and my chest tightened with anxiety, as I squirmed about searching for any possible route of escape. The doors closed and we drove off. I was trapped.

I sat gloomily staring at the cake on my lap, as she wheeled the car sedately into the schoolyard and parked in a prime spot especially reserved for the fair volunteers. I was directed by a robust lady in a floral dress and fancy hat to place the cake on the table with the white cloth. I thought this must be the royal table, as she was definitely the image of the Queen Mother herself.

I milled about with my hands in my pockets and my head hung low, watching my feet shuffle from side to side on the spot, while Mom muttered on and on to several of the other ladies. Suddenly, Mom broke from the herd and walked purposefully towards me. Now what! I thought with anxious anticipation.

"Why don't you run along and meet up with your school chums dear, and would you mind terribly if you walked home with your friends, as I have just volunteered to stay and help clean up."

"No Mom, I don't mind walking home," I sighed with fake disappointment.

"Very well dear, I'll see you at home later. Have fun at the fair." I darted off like a shot, before something changed. I weaved in and out of the thickening crowd, and found Wingnut throwing plastic hoops into a bunch of bottles all nested together. If the hoop landed around one of the necks, the thrower would get a prize.

The entire schoolyard was alive with people, young and old. It was full of tents and stalls of every description. Little kids were overdosing on all manner of sweets, drinks, and assorted treats. Old people were being led by the arm through the crowd, babies were sleeping in their prams, and toddlers were crying in their push chairs as they bawled towards the sky, watching their balloons float off to Mars.

There were several unfortunate people who stood out from the rest, the ones who don't normally get taken out much, but are always taken to the fair.

Wingnut and I lost ourselves, darting from booth to booth, playing every game we came upon. We laughed and joked and had a really good time.

The school bell rang twice, above the hustle, bustle and noise of the fair: Ding! Ding!

"It's twelve o'clock," Wingnut gasped. "Let's go." We zigzagged through the crowd to the back of the school, and disappeared out into the park at full sprint towards the tennis courts. The sun was high in the sky and the heat of the day was emerging. Many people had already left the fair, especially the young, old, and the unfortunate. Many people with cars were already leaving, to simply beat the rush at the end.

We edged the bike out from behind the fence, and we set to work placing all the cardboard boxes in a large semicircle, a short distance from Wingnut's sock tree. I rode off on the armoured bike, across the avenue, and down one of the side streets several blocks, then looped around the back and out onto the avenue. In fifteen minutes, I was in position as planned. I was a little early, so I pushed the bike up one of the small side streets so as not to attract attention, and there I waited, with nervous anticipation.

The school bell rang once. The sound traveled clearly through the hot, still afternoon air; it was one o'clock. Still I waited. It was unusually quiet, no traffic, no people walking; the streets were virtually empty, except for a girl on a bike. It was Samantha, right on time, cruising down the avenue with a blue water balloon jiggling and wobbling about in the bottom of the wicker basket on the front of her bike. I rushed to get into the armoured bike, as she picked up speed and steered off onto the footpath. I rounded the corner and pedaled off after her. As she approached the Shulaks' house, I saw her wobble slightly, as she rode with one hand and picked up the water balloon with the other.

One of the Shulaks was sitting on the wall in front of their house, picking his nose, and nonchalantly eating whatever appeared on the end of his finger. The other one was nowhere in sight. Samantha bravely sped toward their house, with the water balloon poised to throw at the daydreaming bogey eater.

Without warning, the other Shulak came charging out through their broken gate, and flung a large stick at Samantha. It spun furiously, end over end, and struck her hard on the hip. The shock of it sent her careening into the gutter, head first in a tangle of arms, legs, and spinning bike parts. She gathered herself up quickly and ran off across the avenue toward the sock tree, just as I came in between her and the Shulaks. The bogey eater had jumped off the wall, and was carrying a metal pail of choice stones he had gathered to throw at the kids riding home from the fair. The other Shulak had two stolen fire buckets full of hard clods of dirt. He placed them on the ground, and the two of them furiously pelted me with a hail of stones and hard clumps of earth. I pedaled steadily into the raining projectiles. The stones whacked into the side of the bike with a deafening crack. One of the clods of dirt smashed into the wire mesh; it was so hard it didn't break. I felt the clod slam the wire against my foot. The rotating pedal caught on the wire and jammed in mid-cycle. Panic overwhelmed me as the stones and clods continued to hammer and thump against the sides of the bike, in a relentless barrage. I was just coasting now, as I frantically stabbed and kicked at the wire mesh in an effort to free the pedal. I heard a snap as the wire broke and the pedal popped free of its grasp. I bent forward and pumped my legs as hard as I could in an effort to pass the Shulaks. The relentless racket had ceased, and I realized that they must have used up all their ammunition.

Whack! A deafening blast stung my ears, and then whack, another resonating blast. The Shulaks had abandoned their empty buckets, and they were chasing me as I swerved out onto the avenue, and onto the grassy island among the trees. They ran after me, armed with sticks, and were frantically thrashing the sides of the armoured bike, bashing with all their might.

Through the dirt-splattered windshield, I could see the sock tree dead ahead. I was sweating heavily with the effort inside the airless box we had built. Suddenly I realized that I couldn't stop. My brain was buzzing, amid the pounding racket, as the largest Shulak slammed his shoulder against the side of the bike. I swerved out of control and smacked head first into the sock tree. The shell of the bike split open as it bounced off the tree and slammed into the hard, sun-baked ground.

The Shulaks grunted with glee as they set about smashing the wooden shell to pieces with their stout sticks, with me still inside it. They were so intent on their violent frenzy of destruction, that they stopped wide-eyed with their mouths dropped open with surprise when hundreds of half rotten crabapples pelted them from behind, as at least twenty kids swarmed up behind them from their hiding place down street number one.

The Shulaks were panic stricken, as the rain of rotten apples soaked their clothes with brown, stinky juice. Their red hair was full of splattered, dripping, brown, pulpy muck. They spotted a direction of escape and ran off to the right as fast as they could go, only to run into another mob of kids bearing down on them, from side street number two. They were trapped like rats, until they realized that their left side was open. They were ready to bolt again, when the gate to the tennis courts opened and the last group of kids, all armed with objects, appeared before them.

The Shulaks pivoted on the spot, searching frantically in each direction for a means of escape. The only open area that wasn't covered was the gate to the park. The Shulaks spotted the weakness and sprinted for the unmanned park gate. After all the planning and waiting, they were making good their escape.

The Shulaks skidded on the gravel, as they urgently halted their sprint for freedom. The dust rose up from their shoes, and small stones rolled in a little wave ahead of them. They froze on the spot.

As the dust cleared, three boys came striding through the cloud, leading a small band of about ten kids. When they came into view, I recognized them as I crawled out of the wreckage of the bike. It was Ken, Rob and Paul. Somehow they had heard of our plan, and they appeared in the nick of time. The Shulaks were surrounded, and Operation Payback had begun.

All the kids surrounded the Shulaks in a huge, unbroken circle, and hurled ripe and rotten fruit at them, until the ground under their feet was sodden, and so slippery that the whimpering Shulaks could no longer stand up. They had lost all their fight, and their courage had abandoned them. Ken and Rob squelched through the multicoloured mess, followed by Paul, who was carrying a plastic bag. The Shulaks were writhing about in the stinky, gooey mess, whimpering like babies. Ken said,

"Do you remember us?"

"No," one of the Shulaks blubbered.

"Well I will remind you," said Ken firmly, gesturing to Paul to step forward. Paul handed a bag to Ken, who pulled out two strings of ladies stockings all tied together, and handed one to Rob. They set about tying the two Shulaks up in the same fashion as they had had done to them in the lonely field several days earlier.

The circle closed in on the two trussed-up Shulaks, as Ken relayed the story of how the Shulaks had attacked them, tied them up, bound and gagged, and walked off and left them in the middle of the field. One by one the kids in the circle came forward and told the terrified Shulaks how they had felt being attacked by them, and described the damage and trauma they had caused to each one of them. I walked over to the back of the tennis court where I had left the plastic bag I had retrieved from the garage. I returned to the circle, untied the knot in the bag, and slowly poured the contents on the Shulaks' faces. It consisted of two dozen broken eggs that had sat stewing in the bag in the hot sun all day.

Samantha stepped forward and told her story, sharing her feelings about the pain and hurt that the Shulaks had caused her. Then she jammed her hands on her hips, pressed her face into a stern, threatening appearance, and declaring out loud for all to hear, she informed the trussed up captives,

"If anyone at all sees or hears of anyone being attacked or bullied by you Shulaks ever again, you will suffer the same fate, every weekend. Your cruel and evil ways will not be tolerated in any form in this neighbourhood ever again."

She pulled a pocketknife out of her front pants pocket, and slowly opened the glistening blade. She crept slowly towards the wide-eyed Shulaks, and stooped over them as they winced in fear, straining at their bonds and whimpering through the gags around their mouths.

She slit the stockings that bound their hands and feet. She and Ken dragged the defeated Shulaks to their feet, and marched them through a slowly opening gap in the circle. The two cruel bullies slumped off with their tails between their legs.

Operation Payback was over.